Heaton, Shirley

Love will find a
way / Shirley
Heaton

          LP

1858410

WP

LOVE WILL FIND A WAY

When nursing sister Rosie attends to accident victim Sam, they strike up a friendship and, although she is not looking for romance, Rosie finds herself falling in love with him. But her future is clearly mapped out and, realising the relationship cannot continue, she decides to stop seeing Sam. Although a future together seems bleak, Sam is determined to find a way. But can the powers of destiny be challenged?

SHIRLEY HEATON

LOVE WILL FIND A WAY

Complete and Unabridged

LINFORD
Leicester

First published in Great Britain in 2008

First Linford Edition
published 2009

British Library CIP Data

Heaton, Shirley.
 Love will find a way
 - -(Linford romance library)
 1. Nurse and patient- -Fiction.
 2. Love stories. 3. Large type books.
 I. Title II. Series
 823.9'2–dc22

ISBN 978–1–84782–675–6

T. J. International Ltd., Padstow, Cornwall

This book is printed on acid-free paper

1

'Don't let me down, Samir, I beg you.' The words swam around in Sam's brain and refused to disappear. Once more they surfaced and echoed noisily inside his head. How could he deny his father's dying wish?

His mind now in turmoil, Sam was aware he needed a clear head before he reached the office. He realised he must try to blot out those words. As he turned the corner he walked towards the kerb, ready to cross the road. Again the words floated back, and again he tried to drown them. But, before he had the chance to do so, he stepped from the pavement, oblivious of the car coming towards him. The driver braked hard but it was too late. The blare of the horn and the screech of tyres on wet tarmac obliterated the words. Sam lost consciousness.

Weary after a busy night in Casualty, Rosie Khan called out to Sister Wilson, 'See you tomorrow, Trish,' before hurrying from the hospital and heading for the car park. The earlier storm had washed the sky clear of clouds and the warmth of the sun cast its glow above the horizon bringing a faint tinge of colour to her face.

As she stepped into the car and turned the key in the ignition, a smile began to develop and lit up her lovely brown eyes. She patted the seat beside her. She'd bought the trusty little banger four years ago and it had never let her down.

But then a flicker of regret cast a shadow in her mind, and the smile disappeared. Two more months and she would have to let it go. And she would no doubt have to move away.

Quickly dismissing those depressing thoughts, she drove out of the car park and joined the traffic on the busy main road. It was ten past seven in the morning the most hectic time of the day when zombie drivers jostled for position, intent on getting to their destinations on time. Rosie gazed ahead hoping she would be back in time for her daily power-walk with her friends.

It was then she spotted him standing there, apparently ready to cross the road, a tall man with handsome good looks and a head of very dark wavy hair. But he had a sort of blank look about him, a look that told her he lacked concentration and that he was unaware of what was happening around him.

As the traffic lights changed to green, Rosie gently pressed her foot on the accelerator and edged forward. It was then everything seemed to happen in slow motion, and she was powerless to stop the sequence of events. A loud gasp escaped her lips and she felt her heart thud in her chest as the man stepped from the pavement right in front of an oncoming car.

The driver braked to avoid him but the car spun around at ninety degrees on the wet road, narrowly missing a lorry but hitting the dark-haired man full-on with the rear end of his car. His victim fell to the ground like a helpless puppet.

Momentarily, Rosie stared in horror, but her mind soon alerted to the accident. The traffic had slowed almost to a standstill, the drivers now apparently more interested in gawping aimlessly across the road at the spot where the man was lying motionless, rather than getting to work on time.

Desperate to help, Rosie noticed a bus lay-by only a few yards away. She allowed the car to trickle forward and gradually steered it in there. She turned off the ignition and jumped out of the car, quickly weaving her way through the stationary traffic towards the victim.

By this time several passers-by had gathered and the driver, apparently in a state of shock, was trying to rouse his victim but to no effect.

'Don't move him,' Rosie called out as she dashed to the scene. The crowd edged back when they recognised the dark blue uniform beneath her coat. 'Has anyone called an ambulance?' she asked and someone in the crowd answered, 'Yes.'

Rosie checked the victim's pulse and realised that, although he was unconscious, he was still alive. But she noticed that his right leg was twisted awkwardly beneath him, and there was blood trickling from a gash at the side of his head. Quickly rummaging through her bag, she pulled out a clean cotton scarf and gently swabbed the cut before slipping off her coat and spreading it over him. Someone handed her a rolled-up jacket, and she carefully lifted the man's head and slid the jacket beneath it.

Seconds later he opened his eyes and stared intensely for a long hard moment. His pupils were dark, the irises finely encircled in black. It was as though he was penetrating her gaze. And then he seemed to drift away and his eyelids closed.

By this time an ambulance had

drawn up beside Rosie, and two attendants hurriedly stepped out. She recognised them from the previous evening when they'd brought a child into Casualty with severe burns.

'Oh, it's you again, love,' one of them called out to her. 'There's no rest for the wicked,' he continued and laughed at his own words. But as he approached the victim his face became serious. 'Now, what have we here?'

She pulled herself to her feet. 'It's a fractured femur I'd say. Look at the position of the leg,' Rosie told him. 'And he has rather a bad gash on his head. I've checked the pulse and . . . ' she started, but the second attendant, tall and straight-faced, didn't allow her to finish.

'That's OK,' he said, cutting her off abruptly. 'There's no need for you to hang around. We'll sort it from here.'

His brusqueness didn't surprise Rosie. She recalled the previous evening when he'd obviously thought himself very much the Romeo, sidling up to her in Casualty with his chat-up line. But to no avail. It hadn't worked with Rosie, simply because he had a kind of arrogance about him that she disliked. Afterwards he'd strode away defiantly. It was obvious he wasn't used to being rebuffed.

And that set her off again. What sort of man was her type? She had yet to meet her soul-mate and, so far, no-one fitted the bill.

As she removed her coat from the victim and began to slip it back on ready to cross the road to her car, the first attendant called out, 'Lucky you were around, love. I think he'll pull through.'

Rosie turned and smiled before dodging the traffic and climbing back into her car.

$\star$ $\star$ $\star$

'Hi, Rose!' Katie was still back at the house the two of them shared. 'You're later than usual,' she added.

'I was held up — a car accident at Dawes Corner. A man was knocked down — his leg was badly broken,' Rosie explained.

Katie sighed. 'Poor soul,' she murmured. 'But how do you manage it, Rosie? You always seem to be around when accidents happen.'

'I know what you mean,' Rosie replied, recalling the victim's face quite clearly, but it was overshadowed by the image of the ambulance attendant who'd snubbed her.

'But lucky you were there on this occasion. Had someone called an ambulance?'

'They had, but the car driver was dazed and he was trying to pull the poor man off the road,' Rosie continued, her tone and expression filled with emotion. 'Fortunately, it wasn't long before the ambulance turned up.'

'What a relief,' Katie called through from the kitchen. 'I'm just about to make myself a cuppa. Want one?'

'That would go down a real treat,

Katie. But what are you doing still back at home? You're usually off by seven.'

'I've an appointment in the city at nine,' she replied. 'I don't need to leave until a quarter past eight,' she told Rosie as she handed her the tea. 'But I must get out of this,' she added, tugging at her dressing gown, 'and get into something business-like.'

When Katie disappeared to her room Rosie did too. She changed into trainers and jog suit. It was later than usual but she decided to head for the reservoir car park where she hoped to meet up with her friends. She always looked forward to the power-walk. Two circuits of the reservoir took about half an hour, and the exercise tended to dissipate the stress that built up whilst she was in Casualty. Although she was on her feet all day, she enjoyed keeping fit, and this was part of her daily regimen.

Abby and Rick were there when she arrived, Emma too.

'Hi,' Rosie sang out. 'You haven't finished I hope.'

'We haven't started yet. I've just arrived.' Emma bent down to tie her shoe laces.

'Good, then I'm not too late,' Rosie replied.

'No, but you're lucky to have caught us,' Abby chipped in, checking her watch.

'I had to stay with a road accident victim until the ambulance arrived,' Rosie told them. 'I knew I'd be late, but at least I won't be walking alone.'

Rick cut in sharply. 'Rosie, do be careful. I've warned you about walking alone. If there's no-one here, give me a buzz on the mobile. I'm only minutes away. If I can make it, you could wait in the car until I arrive. I don't mind doing a second session and I wouldn't be missed.'

'But you're not always available,' Rosie was quick to respond. 'And I can't always guarantee being here on time.'

'I'm pretty flexible,' Rick told her. 'It's only when I'm taking an early class

I can't make it. And most of my classes start mid-morning.'

'Thanks, Rick. I'll bear that in mind. If Abby's on the same shift as me, that's OK, but Emma's not always about at this time of day.'

'That's right, Rosie. I'm later than usual today. Most times I can manage a quarter to eight but after that I'm pushing it. Today's my day off,' Emma confirmed. 'But Rick's right. Whatever you do, don't walk alone. It's lonely round there.'

'Point taken,' Rosie acknowledged, knowing that if she didn't agree they'd harp on about it forever.

It was well after nine when she finally managed to slide into bed. She was asleep within minutes but she slept restlessly, her dreams a complete jumble of people and places. First it was the accident, the vision of the man lying there helpless, and then it was the rude ambulance attendant.

By four-thirty in the afternoon Rosie was up and about. She made herself a light meal, and afterwards she did a little shopping. Before going back to the hospital, she tried to relax for an hour.

Katie was home for six and they sat down together, as they usually did, to catch up on the day's events.

'How did the meeting go this morning, Katie? Were you on time?' Rosie asked her.

'Only just. It was quite boring actually. We had to listen to a rep going on about his company products.' She smiled. 'But I won't bore you with all that. How did your day go?'

'I've done very little really. I met my friends for the power-walk, came back and went to bed. Nothing exciting, I'm afraid.'

'At least you have your visit to Birmingham at the weekend. You must be looking forward to that.'

'Of course,' Rosie replied, trying not to show her reluctance. 'And Mum and Dad love to see me. But they always harp on about you-know-what,' she added, shaking her head. Whilst she always enjoyed going home to see her parents, there was a little matter they always brought up, something she didn't want to discuss.

It was seven-thirty that evening when Rosie returned to the hospital. But she didn't go straight to Casualty. She had a sudden, fleeting memory of the darkly handsome man at the scene of the accident, and she decided to go along to the orthopaedic ward to check his condition. She called into Sister Gill's office first.

'Last night's accident victim, Margot, the man with the broken leg and head injuries. I take it he's with you.'

'Oh, you mean our lovely Samir,' she replied, her face softening into a smile. 'He's a real sweetiepie, so charming. The nurses adore him. They're bending over backwards to please him.' She paused. 'But lucky you! How do you know him?'

'I witnessed the accident. I stayed with him until the ambulance arrived, that's all.'

'Then that explains it. He's been asking for the nurse who was with him. We were all puzzled,' she said as she got up from her desk and pointed towards Samir's room. 'Would you mind going over and having a word with him? He's been asleep for most of the day but he's wide awake now. Room six, across the corridor.'

'Of course I'll pop across there. But it'll have to be a quickie. I'm due back in Casualty in ten minutes. How is he?'

'He's pulling round. It was a bad break. Mr Rae pinned the fracture,' she explained. 'I'm sure Samir will be pleased to see you.'

Rosie wandered down the corridor until she came to room six, and her gentle knock on the door seemed to startle its occupant who looked up in surprise.

'Oh! It's my lovely nurse,' he said, obviously astonished to see her.

Rosie was taken aback. How on earth did he know who she was? But she smiled and said, 'I'm Rosie. You're

14

Samir, I take it?'

'That's right, Sam to my friends,' he confirmed, his eyes lighting up to a wonderful glow. 'Please sit down, Rosie. I recognised you immediately. You came to my rescue yesterday.' He was softly spoken and polite.

'I'm amazed you remember, Sam. You were really groggy when I caught up with you,' she replied, smiling at his recollection.

'But I could never forget those eyes,' he told her, his own still bright and responsive, signalling his delight that she was there to see him.

Caught in his intense gaze, her heart thudded noisily in her chest and her cheeks began to flush to a pink hue. She couldn't think why. And she struggled to contain her thoughts as she sat on the chair beside his bed.

But pulling herself to her senses, she asked, 'How are you feeling?'

'About you?' he continued, a wicked grin now sketching his face, 'or about this confounded thing?' he asked,

15

tapping the cast on his leg.

'Really!' Rosie replied, shaking her head and laughing. 'I meant the leg, of course.'

He continued to gaze into her eyes and she realised there was something about him that intrigued her. But for goodness sake, what was the matter with her? Surely she'd been affected by nothing more than amusement at his antics, his charms and his chat-up lines. So why was she doing this she asked herself? Why was she drooling over someone she'd spoken to for less than ten minutes? And what was the point? She knew she must stop her foolish behaviour. It would come to no good in the end.

Sam picked up the threads again. 'At least they've pinned it back together.' He paused, gazing intently towards her. But she gave no response. He continued to stare and then he began to frown. 'Did you hear what I said?' he asked. 'You seem to be miles away.'

Suddenly realising that Sam had

been talking in a vacuum whilst she'd been day-dreaming, she stuttered, 'I'm sorry. I didn't mean to be rude. But, yes, I did hear you, Sam.'

'It should start to mend now — the leg I mean. But it's so boring being in here.'

'You'll be out before you know it,' Rosie promised, 'but you'll need to learn to use the crutches before they'll consider discharging you.'

'I'll need help with that,' he urged, winking cheekily. 'Perhaps you could show me the ropes when they let me out of this dratted bed.'

'You're a pushy one, I'll say that for you,' Rosie told him as she stood up to leave, her face once more becoming flushed as Sam grinned back boyishly.

'Only with certain people,' he assured her, a faint trace of amusement in his eyes. 'You will come and see me again, won't you?'

'Of course I will. But Sister Wilson's going to kill me if I don't get down to Casualty quick sharp. I'm supposed to be on duty in a couple of minutes.'

Sam took hold of her hand. 'I'm looking forward to seeing you again. I've so much to thank you for.' He squeezed her hand gently.

She tugged her hand away girlishly. 'I know your sort,' she said, laughing. 'But I'll be back, I promise.'

2

Sam certainly hoped Rosie would be back. But his priority now would be to learn how to handle the crutches once they were available. The sooner he became mobile, the sooner he could be out of this place. He could then arrange to meet up with Rosie. Maybe he could take her out to dinner and thank her properly. That would be so satisfying. He felt the need to spend quality time with her, for them both to relax and get to know each other better.

His reverie was interrupted when one of the junior nurses came into his room, smiling and eager to please. 'Time for physio, Sam. The porter's coming to collect you any minute. Is there anything you need before you go down there?'

'Nothing I can think of,' he told her.

'Will I need my work-out kit?' he asked, rolling his eyes and grinning.

'You're not going down for that sort of exercise. The physio might give you a few exercises to strengthen your muscles whilst you're lying on your bed, nothing more at this stage.'

'I thought they might give me a pair of crutches and show me how to walk,' he dared to offer jokingly, but as the nurse opened her mouth to retaliate, no doubt with some equally smart reply, the porter entered the room.

Sam turned to him. 'Oh, you're here,' he said, reverting his gaze to the nurse. 'It looks as though I'd be too late if I did want anything. I'm to be whisked off somewhere and made to co-operate, jump through hoops at everyone's whim,' he added, smiling.

'You'll be doing anything but jumping through hoops young man,' Sister Gill chipped in as she was passing his room. 'Now do as Nurse Warwick tells you. It's time you behaved yourself,' she concluded as she continued down the corridor, shaking her head and smiling to herself.

'She's a bright spark for a Sister,' Sam observed. 'Nothing like the stereotype.'

'And what is the stereotype, Sam?' the nurse asked him.

'Straight-faced and acid-tongued,' came his deadpan reply.

'Don't let Sister Gill hear you saying that. She's a real good sport, nothing like the image you have in your head. And if that's what you think, where does Sister Khan fit in?'

'Sister Khan? Who's Sister Khan?'

'You mean to tell me you have a visitor and you don't know who she is?'

'Do you mean Rosie?'

'Of course I do.'

'Is she a Sister?' he asked with disbelief etched on his face.

'A junior Sister.' The nurse shook her head and frowned. 'Straight-faced and acid-tongued you say? Perhaps she should know what you think.' The nurse grinned as she collected the case notes from the bottom of the bed and followed the porter down the corridor.

'Don't you dare,' Sam threatened playfully. 'In any case, I've changed my mind. All Sisters are beautiful, and silver-tongued!'

When Sam arrived at the physio-therapy department, he was far from happy. One or two leg raising exercises on the bed, nothing more. And in view of his other injuries, he wasn't allowed to start his practice with the crutches, not for a few more days. After all there was his work to consider.

The new post at Bickerdyke & Wagstaff awaited him. He'd joined the company as an associate member and had been promised a junior partnership after a couple of years, once he'd established himself of course. He'd spent less than three weeks there and had begun to settle in quite nicely, but now here he was stuck in this place when all he wanted was to get started on the cases he'd been allocated.

And he'd been carrying his business

papers in his briefcase when the accident happened. But so far the case hadn't turned up. There were important documents in there, strictly confidential ones. He already had half a dozen cases to deal with, mainly criminal offences, which were his speciality.

Once he was back on the ward he asked to have a word with Sister Gill. 'It's about my briefcase, Sister,' he said. 'I wonder if, the next time you see Sister Wilson in Casualty, you'd ask if my briefcase has turned up yet. I know you've already made enquiries, but it's becoming very much a priority now. The notes in there are confidential.'

'Sorry, Sam, I meant to tell you, but you've beaten me to it. Sister Wilson rang not ten minutes ago. She's asked around and she's finally traced the case to one of the treatment rooms in Casualty. Apparently the cleaning staff had come across it but they thought it belonged to one of the doctors.'

'That's great news, Sister.'

'She'll send it down with a porter as

soon as one of them has a minute to spare,' she announced. She was about to leave the room when she added, 'By the way a Mr Jeremy Brownwell rang whilst you were in physio. He wants you to ring him back. Would you like one of the nurses to wheel the public phone in for you?'

'I'd be really grateful if I could use the phone. Any time when it's convenient, there's no hurry.'

Sam spoke to Jeremy Brownwell, one of the junior partners in the company.

'We heard you'd been involved in an accident, Sam. There was an item on the local news. Now is there anything you need?'

'I'm hoping not to be in here very long, Jeremy.'

'I don't know about that. According to the Sister you suffered quite a serious fracture. But I'll tell you what,' Jeremy suggested, 'I'll pop into your flat and make sure everything is in order there. And since you're new to the area, the boss has asked me to make arrangements for a woman to go in and tidy the place up for you. That's if you agree, of course.'

'What a good idea. I'd appreciate the place being spick and span when I return.'

As he replaced the receiver, one thought triggered another and he wondered if Rosie had a flat of her own. Or did she still live with her parents? She wasn't married — at least if she was she didn't wear a ring. But he'd check things out when next he saw her, subtly of course.

* * *

Her day shift complete, Rosie was ready to leave and the image of Sam lying in the hospital bed swam in perfect detail into her vision. She was so close to the orthopaedic ward, maybe she could pop down there and see him again. He had asked her to visit him, and it seemed a pity not to do so. But she hesitated, stalling for time before making a decision.

A deep sigh trickled through her. It might seem a bit over the top visiting him so soon after the first visit and, for that reason, she kept on screwing up the courage to go along there. After all they'd only just met and she didn't want him to think she was overly forward, although she was anxious to check that he was improving.

Her decision made, she left the hospital and headed for the car park. She may as well get back home, change and leave for the reservoir. Afterwards she would put her feet up for a couple of hours, maybe chill out and watch television.

The car was in her sights as she took the keys from her bag. But then she paused, and a kind of tenderness began to flow through her when she thought of Sam. And she couldn't help feeling a sense of regret that she'd decided not to visit him. But still she hovered, keys poised.

Decisions could be overturned. It

was time for plan B. She spun briskly around and left the car park, returning to the building and heading for the orthopaedic ward.

Sam had a heap of papers on his bed when she turned the corner into room six, and her gentle tap on the door broke his concentration. The minute he looked up she saw the delight leap into his eyes, his enthusiasm heart-warming.

'Great to see you again, Rosie. But you're looking tired.' He patted the chair beside the bed. 'Come, sit down and talk to me,' he said, his tone soft and persuasive.

'It hasn't taken you long to settle in,' Rosie laughed. 'And what are you hoping to do with that lot?' she asked him, sitting down and pointing to the pile of papers.

'I had them with me at the time of the accident but they disappeared temporarily. Good old Sister Gill managed to retrieve them from Casualty. They're my case files. I've already started to read them through,' he said, patting his laptop computer. 'I may as well do the spadework whilst I'm in here.'

'Are you allowed to use that in here, Sam?' she asked, pointing to the computer and shaking her head in amazement.

'I'm not allowed to go online,' he told her. 'They'll let me use it, but only in my own room on battery, to update my files. It'll need a re-charge when the battery runs down. And before you ask, I do have Sister Gill's permission,' he added emphatically, giving a nod of the head and smiling.

'It's just as well. You need to keep in her good books,' Rosie replied, smiling back at him. 'But what exactly is your job, Sam?'

'I'm a solicitor, mainly working on criminal cases. My job entails a lot of investigation. I can't afford to make mistakes.'

'I understand, Sam.' She got up from the chair. 'But maybe you'd like to get on with your work. I didn't mean to disturb you.' Perhaps she shouldn't have visited after all.

'There's no way you're disturbing me, Rosie. I have all the time in the world to read these through whilst I'm in here,' he stressed, picking up the piles of papers and slotting them into an envelope file.

'How have things gone since I saw you, Sam?' she asked him.

'Disappointing to say the least. I'm not allowed to try the crutches, not for another day or so.'

'I'm not surprised. You must be careful not to strain your leg too much. It's not worth it. Hang on in there. It won't be for long.'

'You stick together you lot,' he said, shaking his head and smiling an easy, confident smile. And then changing the subject he asked, 'Are you on the same shifts all the time?'

'No, we change shifts regularly. We have a roster.'

'That's good. I'd like us to go out for a meal sometime soon.'

'Out for a meal?' Rosie laughed. 'You don't waste much time, do you?'

'I don't have time to waste. I'll be back to my job once I'm discharged from this place. I'm new to the area and, as yet, I haven't had the chance to meet many people. We've broken the ice you and I — through unusual circumstances I know — so why not build on our friendship? And most of all I want to thank you for saving my life.'

'Saving your life?' Rosie laughed out loud. 'That's the best excuse I've heard in a long time.' She felt herself flush with pleasure. 'As for people to thank, that makes it me, the ambulance crew, Sister Gill and the nurses on orthopaedics — in total that is,' she said, counting them on her fingers and taking a deep breath. 'Don't forget you've broken the ice with them through similar circumstances. Are they invited too?'

'You're joking of course. And they're different.'

'In what way?'

He hesitated for a moment and then he said, 'They haven't got that . . . ' He paused and then he added, 'You know, that appeal.'

'You're brilliant with chat-up lines, I'll give you that. But don't forget you're still ensconced in here, and not likely to be out for some time.'

He drew a deep breath. 'I'll wait until I'm out of here and then you must promise you'll let me treat you to dinner.'

Rosie consulted her watch. 'I've arranged to do a couple of circuits around the reservoir with my friends,' she told him, realising it was getting quite late. 'I'm hoping they'll still be there,' she added, standing up ready to leave. 'I have stayed longer than I intended.'

'Circuits around the reservoir? Jogging, you mean?' he asked.

'Power-walking actually. It's the best way I know to keep the cardiovascular system strong and healthy.'

Sam pulled himself up on the bed,

shrugged his shoulders and grinned. 'I see,' he said, reaching out and glancing briefly towards the door before taking her hand. 'I do admire a healthy woman,' he added, pulling her towards him and gently kissing her on the cheek. 'Enjoy, and come back soon,' he begged, 'promise.'

'Promise,' she said, arching her eyebrows and turning her twinkling eyes towards his, her heart beating a rapid tattoo after that gentle kiss.

And Sam watched her with total absorption. 'Tomorrow?' he asked, his eyes conveying his silent plea.

'Just as soon as I can,' she concluded, not wanting to commit herself, as she waved and left the room.

Are things getting too much to handle? she asked herself. But what was the solution? Staying away, she supposed.

It was later than she expected when she reached the reservoir, by which time none of her friends were about. They'd obviously completed the walk and left. Usually they met at five-thirty and although it wasn't much after six, she'd missed them. Had she met them before they'd completed the circuits, Rick would have stayed with her.

She looked around. It was still light and she reckoned that if she set off immediately she could complete the two circuits in half-an-hour and be back home well before darkness fell.

The sun was golden in the washed blue stretch of sky, and the breeze was soft and warm on her skin as Rosie set out at a steady pace, breathing in the fresh air and feeling invigorated. It was good to be alive.

An elderly couple came towards her with two Yorkshire terriers, and a young boy on a bike pedalled past her. It was obvious Rick and the gang had over-reacted when they'd gone on about not doing the circuit on her own. There were people around, and there was nothing to be afraid of.

Four swans, a flock of mallards and several Canada Geese, which was unusual for the time of year, swam about on the reservoir. And Rosie became so engrossed in watching their antics that, at first, she didn't hear the footsteps behind her. But gradually the faint squeak of rubber soles on the footpath became louder. And there was something about the footsteps that alarmed her. It was as though someone was sneaking up behind her.

Her heart began to beat faster and anxiety overcame her. Only seconds ago there'd been the couple with the dogs, and the boy on the bike. But now they'd all disappeared.

Tentatively she turned. Her stomach gave a hefty somersault as she glimpsed the figure of a man dressed in dark clothing. He was wearing black trainers and some sort of balaclava which, apart from two slits for the eyes, completely covered his face. No sooner had she spotted him than he spun around and swiftly dodged into the nearby bushes, disappearing so quickly she didn't get a chance to see him clearly.

Momentarily her legs turned to jelly. She seemed to lose all strength and was unable to move. But within seconds she started to run, realising she had a long way to go before she reached the car park.

By the time she'd passed the half way point she'd put on such a spurt she was quickly becoming exhausted. She was breathing heavily now but still she kept on looking around. There was no sign of the man, either on the path behind her or lurking in the bushes. He could be anywhere. He could have made his way behind the bushes and be ahead of her now.

Anxious to get back to the safety of her car, she pressed on.

But a stitch pain in her side was beginning to trouble her, and she needed to stop for a breather. She bent over and took in heavy gulps of air, shaking her head to clear the myriad questions bombarding her mind. Why was she being followed? Why had the man disappeared into the bushes? Was he intent on frightening her or would he attack?

At the sound of rustling, she straightened up and turned, once more catching a brief glimpse of the man, who was now peering through the bushes. Her stomach continued its roller-coaster and, again, the incident was so fleeting that it would have been impossible for her to identify the man.

Still out of breath, she set off running again, but more slowly this time in an effort to pace herself. She still had a fair way to go and she knew for certain he was following her. Would she make it to the car park?

But she'd gone no more than a hundred yards when the stitch pain returned, and she was forced to stop again. This time she turned and faced the direction in which the stalker had pursued her, straining her eyes to look through the bushes. As far as she could see, there was no-one in sight.

After a couple of minutes walking the pain continued, but still she tried to set off running again, realising she must move on before he came out into the open and caught up with her.

As she did so the heavy, plodding squeak of rubber soles on the footpath startled her. They were coming closer and closer, and her stomach began to churn even more aggressively. This was it. Now the stalker was out in the open, and ready to attack.

'Is something wrong?' came a call from behind her. 'You're looking worried.' Rosie turned and immediately recognised the dark green T-shirt of the countryside warden.

She caught her breath, and a sigh of relief escaped her lips. 'Someone's been following me. A man came up behind as though to attack me, goodness knows why,' she replied, looking back down the path to check if he was still about. 'But then he dodged into the bushes.'

'I thought you looked upset. I've just come through the gap in the bushes from the park. I didn't see anyone.'

'Whoever it was came from the

bushes too, but further back.'

'Had you seen him before?'

'I wouldn't have been able to tell. He was well disguised, dressed in dark clothes, black I think, and he was wearing some sort of balaclava. He was really sinister.'

'So there was nothing familiar about him?'

'Nothing at all.'

'Anything else about him you can remember, his height, his weight — anything like that?'

'He was quite tall and fairly slim, but that's all I can tell you.'

'At least that's something to go on,' he offered. 'We've always felt it was safe around here, but you can't be too careful. I know nothing significant happened, but he did scare you. Don't walk alone again, love.' He took a notebook from his pocket. 'If you care to give me your name I'll support your complaint. I was witness to part of it, although I didn't actually see the man.'

'But what good will that do? I

wouldn't recognise him again.'

'That aside. I need to report it.'

'My name is Rosina Khan,' she told him. 'I usually meet my friends to do the walk but I was late today and they'd all left.'

'I would normally say that was OK, but after what you've experienced, I have my reservations.' He moved closer and bent his head to scribble her name in his notebook.

Rosie stared at the top of his head, noticing that his hair was an untidy mass. It was badly ruffled which she thought rather strange. Usually the rangers were smart. And another thing he was wearing black trainers when she thought walking boots would have been more appropriate. A tiny niggle at the pit of her stomach triggered off a nasty feeling.

But she was being silly. The warden seemed too concerned for her welfare to be under suspicion.

The warden cut into her thoughts and she had no more time to speculate.

'Now then, Rosina, I can see you're upset, exhausted too by the look of you. How are you getting home?'

'I left my car in the car park over there,' she said, pointing to it and edging further away.

'I'll walk you to the car just to make sure you're safe. Do take care in the future.'

She summoned up the courage to reply. 'I can assure you I don't intend walking alone again.' She paused. 'And thanks.'

Katie hadn't returned when Rosie reached the flat and she was still feeling shaky. More than anything she was puzzled as to why anyone would want to scare her.

She moved to the kitchen but, by now, she'd completely lost her appetite. Her best plan would be to take a relaxing bath and have an early night. But she would need to wait until Katie returned before bolting the door for the night. She turned the key in the lock and removed it. At least if Kate returned whilst she was in the bath she'd be able to get in without disturbing Rosie.

The bath was a comfort, and she luxuriated in its warmth, allowing herself to drift into dreamland, and Sam came to the forefront of her mind. But then her stomach churned when she thought about the stalker. Rick had been right after all. She must never walk alone again. And whilst she didn't want to lose face and confess what had happened, only to be given the 'I told you so' reply, she felt Abby and Emma should be told.

They should be warned against walking alone.

As she lay there relaxing she heard a gentle knocking noise which made her jump. Was that someone at the door?

Now she was being edgy. And that was silly. She was locked up securely in her own house. But the knock was repeated.

Who could it be at this time of night? Perhaps she should ignore it. But what if it was important?

She stepped out of the bath and slipped her arms into her bath robe and tied it tightly around her. As she advanced towards the door, the knock came again, louder this time.

'I'm coming,' she called out as she slid the chain guard across for safety and unlocked the door, inching it open and looking outside through the slit.

But there was no-one there.

She closed the door again and went to the window, checking the garden and the front path to the door. Still there was no-one in sight. But whoever it was could be hiding, lying in wait until either she went outside or Katie returned.

Intent on ringing Katie to warn her, Rosie dashed into the kitchen and picked up the phone. She dialled the number and waited. There was no reply and Katie's voicemail clicked on. Katie's phone was either switched off or out of signal range. Rosie left a message.

She stood there for some time, absently gazing through the window and then staring at the phone. But still Katie didn't ring.

What was happening to her? First it was the stalker and now a mysterious caller. Maybe it was a coincidence. But whoever it was had certainly set out to unnerve her.

3

Rosie had a busy day at work. When she'd finished her shift she decided to call in at the police station on her way home and report the incident at the reservoir. In normal circumstances she probably wouldn't have bothered, but since the warden seemed anxious to protect other people who visited the reservoir, especially the children who played there, she supposed she was right in doing so. But she wouldn't mention her suspicions about the warden.

The police station was empty when she arrived, and she rang the bell at the front desk. The duty sergeant came bustling out and asked if he could help her.

'It's a strange thing to report,' she said, a frown appearing on her forehead, 'because nothing really happened.'

'Nothing happened?' he repeated, looking puzzled. 'You're right. That is a strange thing to report.'

'I don't exactly mean nothing happened, but it didn't come to anything.' The sergeant continued to look puzzled. 'I think someone was stalking me. I went to the reservoir early yesterday evening and that was when it happened. But no harm's been done. He didn't attack me or anything like that.' She gave the sergeant as much detail as she could, together with her limited description of the man.

'Have you had problems before, you know, this sort of thing?' he asked her. 'Do you know of anyone with a grudge against you?'

'I've never experienced anything like this before, and I don't know of anyone with a grudge. But another thing which may be completely unrelated, someone knocked on my door a couple of hours later whilst I was in the bath, and when I got out, they'd gone. I found that quite strange too after the stalking.'

'I don't see anything unusual about that, Miss Khan. By the time you got yourself out of the bath, whoever it was probably thought you were out.'

'I don't think so because just as I was about to put on the chain guard and open the door, whoever it was knocked again.'

'I see. That is rather odd, I must say. The stalking ties in with what Ian Grice, the countryside warden, reported.'

'The countryside warden? He reported it?' she asked, her voice almost rising to a crescendo.

'You sound surprised, Miss. He said he'd witnessed some of what happened but he didn't actually see the man, if it was a man. It could have been a woman for all we know.'

'It definitely wasn't a woman. The stalker had a man's build.'

'Grice came in yesterday afternoon, told us all about it. He's always concerned for the kids who play there.' The sergeant took out a pad from beneath the desk. 'I'll make out a report

46

and send a constable down there, see if he can come up with anything. Meanwhile, take care. I'm sure you know all the rules about safety,' he warned.

'I certainly do, and I realise it was foolish of me to go alone.'

'You've learnt your lesson,' he added with a smile. 'Leave it with us, Miss. We'll look into it.'

Rosie left the police station, her mind buzzing with the incident of the stalker. And it seemed that her suspicions about the warden were completely unfounded. He wouldn't have reported the incident had he been the stalker.

Her mind turned to Sam. Should she visit him today? But she realised he was getting a little too familiar and she needed to cool things. Decision made. She would give him a miss tonight. She'd call in and see him tomorrow night. After all she didn't want to become too involved. Not that she didn't enjoy the innocent banter, but she didn't want to mislead him into thinking there might be something between them when she knew that was out of the question.

Katie was there when Rosie returned to the house and, whilst Rosie had mentioned nothing the previous day about either the incident at the reservoir or the caller, she felt she needed to tell Katie now.

'You must be crazy. Your friends were right. I certainly wouldn't walk around the reservoir path alone,' Katie stressed, shaking her head. 'But what was the guy like?'

'The description I gave the police is very basic, Katie. He was well disguised.'

'You'd be better joining the health club in my opinion than taking the chance on your friends being around when you get to the reservoir.'

'Oh, I don't know, Katie. If there's no-one around in the future I'll give Rick a buzz. He's not very far away and he told me that, if I was stuck he'd meet me, provided he was free of course. He said he doesn't mind doing a double session.'

'But he's not forced to be available. It's all hit and miss, if you ask me. If you want regular exercise, for goodness sake, join the gym.'

'It's not as easy as that. Even if I joined the club, it would be difficult when I'm on shifts. As for the power walking, when I'm on nights or middle shift it's OK. But I can't make the mornings when I'm on earlies.'

'Suit yourself, love. But take care.' Katie appeared to hesitate for a moment and then she added, 'I don't understand why someone should be knocking at the door though. That's rather strange. Are you sure you heard someone?'

'I'm positive. They knocked three times. I tried to ring you on your mobile to warn you someone may be hanging about outside when you returned, but either your phone was switched off or you were out of area. I did leave a message.'

'I've obviously not checked my messages,' Katie confessed. 'I was in a meeting. I'd switched it off deliberately,' she confirmed. 'I forgot to switch it on again before I left.'

She sat down on the sofa and folded her arms. 'But it's scary, Rosie. Maybe there was no connection between the stalker and the caller. Maybe it was nothing but coincidence,' Katie offered, a false air of optimism to her voice.

'You could be right, but why did the person disappear when I opened the door?'

'Search me,' Katie continued. 'We must be careful from now on. But why didn't you tell me all this yesterday.'

'You were late. I'd gone out before you returned and when I came home you were already in bed, remember.'

'Of course, I do now that you mention it. But let me know if anything else happens that seems suspicious.'

★ ★ ★

It was Friday and Rosie finished her shift promptly. She decided to go straight to the reservoir and meet her friends for the walk. That would give her time afterwards, before she went to bed for a few hours rest, to pack her overnight bag in preparation for her trip to the Midlands. It was her weekend off and she was looking forward to visiting her parents in Birmingham.

She hadn't been to the reservoir since the evening she was followed, and she felt a little apprehensive as she drew up in the car park. Abby and Emma were already there and Rick arrived minutes later. 'How about that? We're all here together, for once.' He smiled and then he added, 'I've had some wonderful news. I've been promoted to fully-fledged lecturer.'

'But I thought you were that already,' Abby ventured.

'My post was assistant lecturer, Abby. There's a big difference,' he added, his smile lighting up his face.

'Congratulations, Rick,' Rosie and

Emma chorused.

'Yes,' Abby offered. 'You've done well considering you're only twenty-six.'

'I am pleased, I must say,' Rick told them. 'And what have you lot been up to?' he continued in a mock superior manner, and they laughed heartily.

'Remember the accident I told you about,' Rosie replied. 'I've been to see the man who was knocked down.'

'Is he OK now?' Emma asked.

'Yes, he's doing fine,' she replied a little coyly. 'Well, he's more than OK, he's quite dishy really.'

'Be careful, Rosie. Don't get too involved,' Abby said playfully, and she began to laugh. Emma joined in but Rick turned away and seemed to ignore the comment.

Then he interjected. 'Come on. Let's get cracking. We don't want to stand around all day,' he ventured and strode out in front at a brisk pace. The other three caught up and, interspersed with deep breaths, they continued their conversation about Rick and his promotion.

With the light-heartedness of the conversation, Rosie didn't want to put a damper on things, and she decided not to mention the stalking incident until the next time they met.

The walk complete, she returned to the flat, packed and went to bed for an hour or two. It was early afternoon when she left Leeds for the Midlands, in plenty of time to avoid the bulk of the peak traffic.

The evening meal was ready when Rosie arrived at her parents' house.

'Rosina, darling, we've missed you,' Serina Khan took her daughter's hands and drew her close, giving her a hug. 'How are things at the hospital?'

'They're going well, Mum. You've no idea how much I enjoy my job.'

'But you realise you won't be there much longer,' her father said, 'and then you'll have no need to go out to work. Not straight away.'

'But, Dad, I love my job in Leeds.'

'I'm sure there'll be something in Birmingham,' he insisted, 'later on, of course. And we like you here with us. I'm not happy knowing you live alone.'

'But she's not on her own, Asad,' her mother pointed out.

'That's right, Mum. I have Katie to keep me company.'

It was always a battle when she visited them and she always came away with a churning stomach. And she knew why. It was a battle of wills. They had made plans for her future, plans she kept on casting from her mind in the hope that she could ignore them. But it couldn't go on for much longer. There would come a day when she'd have to face up to things.

The weekend seemed to fly by. Rosie loved going back to see her parents and they were delighted to see her. She was an only child and every time she went back home they wanted her to stay. But this time there was no getting away from it. Her parents had certain expectations and whether she liked it or not, she must try her best to see their reasoning, and conform to their wishes.

★ ★ ★

It was three days before Rosie met up with Sam again. Monday was the start of her night shifts but she didn't have time to go along in the evening. Instead she called in on him at seven o'clock in the morning when the shift was over.

She tip-toed down the corridor to the room, just in case he was still asleep.

The first thing she noticed was the pair of crutches propped up in the corner of the room behind his locker. Sam heard her enter and he pulled himself up in the bed.

'I'm awake,' he whispered.

'I see you've used your persuasive charms to get your own way,' she observed, keeping her own voice down and pointing to the crutches. 'Either that, or your campaign of attrition has worked.'

'I don't know what you mean,' Sam replied with a chuckle.

'I may only have known you for a

week or so, but don't think I haven't noticed how you manage to wheedle things out of people,' she added, a smile springing to her lips.

'You've got it all wrong, Rosie. I was ready for the crutches. They admitted that down in physio.' His face was a picture of naivety.

'Only when you pushed your luck with them. Don't think I haven't spoken to Melanie. She's a sucker for a charmer.'

Sam started to laugh. 'A charmer? You don't know me at all,' he claimed. 'But if you agree to have dinner with me on Thursday, you could get to know me better.'

Rosie shook her head. 'You've got a nerve, asking me out when you've no idea when you'll be discharged.'

'I'm working on that one. I'll be there. Just watch me go on these crutches.'

'Not so quick, Sam,' Rosie interjected, holding up her hand. 'I don't want to be responsible if you fall.'

'Don't worry I wouldn't sue. I'd expect a different kind of compensation,' he stressed and his face softened into a smile.

Something in the gentleness of his tone touched her. How could she possibly reprimand him when he looked at her like that? A happy smile lit up her face.

'OK, you win. I'll have dinner with you, but I'm not prepared to agree to any arrangements until you're ready to leave.'

'Suits me,' he added. 'Now what have you been up to over the weekend?'

'I went down to see my parents in Birmingham. I try to go at least once a month. They gave up a lot for me to go to university and then complete my probationary time in hospital, not to mention their financial support. I owe them a great deal. And I love them dearly. They're the only close relatives I have here in England, apart from an elderly uncle who lives in the next street.' Rosie sat down on the chair beside the bed.

'Why did you choose Leeds?' Sam asked her. 'It seems a long trek going back to the Midlands on a regular basis. I would have thought there'd have been a job closer to home. Isn't there supposed to be a shortage of qualified nurses?'

'Yes, there is a shortage. And, yes, there were plenty of jobs closer to home. But not in Casualty. I'm Junior Sister now. I was lucky to be accepted only three years after completing my training, but I wanted to gain promotion as quickly as possible,' she told him, not wishing to explain her reasoning.

'You're an ambitious one, I'll say that. But I'm glad you didn't stick with your parents, otherwise I'd never have met you.' He paused and slipped his legs out of the bed. 'Now watch me closely and see how skilled I am.'

He slotted his hands through the circular arm rests and set out across the room, but Rosie couldn't help noticing his valiant attempt to hide his apprehension with a strained smile. And she cringed inwardly, feeling a niggle of anxiety as she sat stiffly on the chair beside the bed. After all it wasn't long since the accident, and here he was cavorting around in the ward as though his life depended on it. He turned, came back towards her and then he eased his weight on to the bed.

'How about that?' he asked, his look of apprehension replaced by a smug grin.

'You show off! I bet you have all the nurses twisted around your little finger, watching you parade around the ward,' she replied, a sigh of relief escaping her lips now that it was over. 'But do take care, Sam. I'm not joking. Don't overdo it.'

★   ★   ★

The squeaking of crepe soles on the highly polished floor signalled that one of the nurses was on her way. But it wasn't one of the nurses. It was Sister Gill. Fortunately he was behaving when she entered his room.

'With luck we might have you out of here by tomorrow afternoon. Mr Rae will be here some time in the morning — he's usually early — and he'll probably discharge you, provided you stick to the rules and show him that you can manage the crutches — without trying to run, of course.'

'Indeed, Sister. I wouldn't dream of overdoing it. I know my limitations,' he assured her pompously, but she obviously didn't miss the way his mouth relaxed and the smile that began to spread across his lips.

'You'll tell me anything, Sam,' she countered and her own half smile developed fully. 'Now down to the nitty gritty. Who have you at home to take care of you?'

The question floored him. He was up against it now. He had no-one at home, but he was keen to get back to work as soon as possible, crutches and all.

However, he wasn't going to tell her that.

'I have a very accommodating land-lady,' he told her. That was true but it wasn't to say she'd look after him.

'But is she on the spot? Does she live in the same building?'

'She's down below on the ground floor.'

'I suppose that's better than nothing. I take it you're on a floor above.'

'Yes, that's right.'

'It's going to be quite a task climbing stairs. You may think you'll manage all right, but it's when you have to go up and down once or twice a day you'll begin to tire.'

'We have a lift, Sister. I wouldn't normally use it, but under the circumstances and since I'm on the first floor, I'll certainly be taking advantage.'

'That's fine, Sam. Now take care and keep your nose clean until Mr Rae turns up tomorrow.' She gave him a long, hard stare and shook her head, and he knew he'd be inordinately sorry if he dared to cross her. And when Sister left his room he wanted to do a little jig. But he was being silly again.

And why did he want to do a little jig? He was going home! But that was not all he wanted. He wanted to see Rosie again and take her out to dinner. He hadn't seen her today and he hoped she'd turn up tonight because he'd need to tell her he might be discharged the next day. If he missed her he might not see her again.

When Rosie arrived at Casualty there was a note waiting for her. It was from Sam and it read: *Good news. Please call in at the ward, ASAP*. Rosie guessed what the good news might be and, since she was early, she decided to call in and see Sam before the shift.

Sister Gill was in her office when she arrived at the orthopaedic ward. 'I hope you're not looking for Sam,' she said.

'Yes, I am, as a matter of fact. Why do you say that? Is something wrong?' Rosie asked, a touch of anxiety in her voice.

'He's left, gone home. Mr Rae came in early this morning and decided he should be discharged — after Sam had demonstrated his walking technique with the crutches, of course.' She folded her arms. 'Sam asked if he could call in at Casualty before he left but when we enquired we realised you were on nights. He's left you an address and phone number. Says he hopes you'll contact him.' She smiled and her eyes were warm with humour. 'Aren't you the lucky one?'

Rosie's stomach took a nosedive. 'I don't know about that, Margot. You know the situation with my parents.'

'You need some quality in your life. Go out and grab it, Rosie. You can't spend your life pandering to someone else's wishes, even though it's what your parents would like. You need some excitement in your life, some fun, before it's too late.'

'I know what you're saying, but you have to understand our culture to realise how important it is to them that

I marry Imran, the man they've chosen for me.'

'But do you want to marry someone you don't know?'

'I suppose not really. My parents have an idea about my feelings. But that's not the point. They say arranged marriages are good because the partners have to work together and learn to love each other, if they want to make a success of it — out of necessity, I suppose.' Rosie sighed. To her these were empty words but she hadn't told her parents so.

They had arranged for her to marry the son of a very good friend of her father's. Rosie hadn't seen the man she was to marry, except for a photograph when he was a young boy. The up-to-date photograph they'd been promised hadn't yet arrived because there had been family problems and her 'intended' had been away from home for some considerable time.

And now Rosie was in a dilemma. Did she call on Sam at his flat and go against her parents' wishes, or did she try to forget all about him? But now wasn't the time to address this issue.

'Thanks for the address, Margot,' Rosie replied, taking the slip of paper from her, 'but I must get back to Casualty. Sister Wilson knows I'm here already.'

'Better not get into her bad books,' Margot concluded, pulling a face. 'Trish can be a bit of a tartar if she's that way out.'

4

The shift complete, Rosie collected her things and went to the car park. For now, she must try to blot out all thoughts of Sam. He'd left and she'd missed him. Was that a let-out for her?

She'd told the others about the stalker and she'd arranged to meet Rick at eight o'clock at the reservoir. The plan was for her to stay in the car until he arrived. Now she needed to get moving, otherwise she'd be late.

He was there before her and they set out along the path at a stiff pace.

'I'm not going to say 'I told you so,' Rosie, but do take care. Promise me you'll never walk alone again.'

'Promise — and this time I mean it. I dread meeting up with the stalker again.'

'Did you get a good description?' he asked her.

'Not really. I wouldn't know him from Adam.'

'Well, there you are. He could easily strike again.'

'Don't worry. I don't intend walking alone again, Rick.'

When the walk was over they set off towards the car park. 'Tomorrow morning? Will it be later, or can you make it at the usual time?' Rick asked her.

'I'm hoping the usual time. I'd like to see the others. Will they be here?'

'I don't see why not. In any case, they know to ring me if either of them is going to be late.'

'Then I'll try my best,' she said, faltering slightly. 'You know, if I don't walk in the mornings when I'm on the nightshift, I don't walk at all.'

'Tomorrow it is then,' Rick replied, and before she knew it he'd taken her hands and popped a gentle kiss on each cheek.

It was then Rosie was filled with a strange feeling of unease. There was something very wrong. And immediately she knew what it was.

It was that scent, the same aroma that had filled the air after the stalker had approached her. She could never forget it. She knew it was familiar, and now she knew exactly why she recognised it. Her stomach churned violently. Who was the stalker? First she'd thought it could be the warden. And now Rick. Surely the stalker couldn't be Rick?

Rosie tried to convince herself that Rick couldn't possibly be the stalker. Surely he wasn't the sort of person who'd do something like that. Or was he? He seemed keen to walk with her. Could that be the reason? Could he have posed as a stalker to discourage her from walking alone, so that she'd walk with him instead?

He had given her a kiss. But that meant nothing. The continental kiss was catching on these days. But he couldn't possibly fancy her when he could easily choose from the glamorous pair Abby and Emma. And this business of the aftershave wasn't necessarily conclusive. After all some of these aftershaves and body sprays were very popular, common even.

This put her in a dilemma. First of all she'd suspected the warden, but then she'd pooh-poohed that idea after he'd called in at the police station and reported the incident. And to add to her confusion now Rick was in the frame.

But she must banish all accusations from her mind. She was clutching at straws. It could be anyone.

As she left the car park her thoughts triggered off another problem. Sam! Rosie desperately wanted to visit him, but for the next few days she must gain the strength to avoid any contact.

She couldn't let her parents down. And if she became attached, things could only get worse. Surely her parents would not willingly agree to her becoming involved with someone other than the chosen one, Imran. So far, they'd been patient with her. But she couldn't procrastinate forever. Time was fast running out.

★   ★   ★

Sam was puzzled as to why Rosie hadn't contacted him. He'd been at home a couple of days now and she hadn't even telephoned. Surely it couldn't be the end. She'd seemed in agreement to their having dinner together the last time they met at the hospital. But of course she could have changed her mind.

He knew he needed to be careful not to put too much strain on his leg, especially when he had an appointment to see Mr Rae again the following week, but he would like to see Rosie again, and soon. Surely there must be something wrong for her not to have telephoned or called in by this time.

He was doing well with the crutches. He'd certainly got the hang of them and, although he'd been forbidden both by Mr Rae and his employers to go back to work until after his check up, it didn't mean he couldn't slip down to Casualty where he hoped to see Rosie.

He'd become so confident, he'd probably done more than he should on the crutches. His leg had been a little painful and was swelling slightly. Whatever happened, he must be very careful. He didn't want to be back in hospital again.

How about if he rang for a taxi to take him there? That would be the best solution. He could be there in five minutes. He had a feeling Rosie would be on duty by ten o'clock, and it would work out well if she could slip out for a few minutes, just to make arrangements for their evening out.

With that in mind, he rang for a taxi and slowly moved out of the apartment towards the lift. Once downstairs, he waited at the outer door for several minutes to rest awhile before going outside to pick up the taxi.

The pain had eased slightly by that

time and he realised it was only by being sensible that his leg would improve.

He stood on the pavement waiting, and after ten minutes he realised something was wrong. He took out his mobile phone and rang again.

'It's Mr Azam. I ordered a taxi at Victoria Apartments but it hasn't turned up.'

'Sorry, sir. There's been an accident in Charles Street. The taxi's on its way now.'

The taxi driver apologised profusely, and held the crutches whilst Sam swung himself into the front passenger seat.

'Thank goodness you've arrived,' Sam told him. 'I need to be at the hospital by ten.'

'I'll have you there in a jiffy,' the driver told him as he wove his way through the busy traffic.

When they reached the hospital, Sam took his time getting out of the taxi. He kept on telling himself he needed to be extra careful. It wouldn't do to slip-up at this stage. He adjusted the crutches and made his way to the front doors of the hospital, heading for Casualty.

The waiting room was full when Sam approached the young girl on reception duty. He hoped Rosie wouldn't be too busy to see him. Surely she could spare a couple of minutes.

'I need to see Rosina Khan, one of the Casualty sisters. It is rather important.'

'You're not here for an appointment then?' the clerk asked him.

'No. That's next week. But I would like to see Sister Khan if she's available.'

'And what's your name?' she asked him.

'Samir Azam,' he replied, 'Sam to my friends,' he added, smiling warmly.

'I'm not supposed to do this,' the young girl told him, 'but let me see, Sister Khan. I'm afraid she's not on duty until this afternoon. She's on late shift today.'

'What time will she be here?'

'She starts at two o'clock. She's usually here for one-thirty.'

'Then I'll get myself a newspaper, read for a couple of hours and wait.'

'There's a cafeteria further along the ground floor if you'd like to grab a coffee. That might pass a bit of time for you,' she advised him, as she leant forward and whispered, 'It's against the rules for me to get involved in arrangements between staff and members of the public, but seeing it's you,' she concluded as she pouted prettily and smiled willingly into his face.

'Thanks for that,' Sam offered, his voice caressing. He was fully aware he could charm his way out of anything, even though he knew it was wrong of him to do so with such an innocent victim.

But it was all in a good cause, so who cared?

By the time one-thirty came around, Sam was back in the waiting room. He began to look towards the door in anticipation, but after half an hour, Rosie hadn't appeared. Where could she be? Surely he hadn't missed her coming through the doors. And then it struck him. Perhaps there was a different entrance.

Sam went back to reception and grinned sheepishly. 'It's me again. Rosie doesn't seem to be around and it's getting late. Is there a different entrance?'

'No. This is the only entrance to Casualty.'

'There's nothing wrong is there? She hasn't rung in to say she's ill or anything like that?'

'Not that I know of,' the girl replied, looking bewildered. 'I can't understand it. She's usually here before now. How about if I pop into the treatment rooms and see if there's any sign of her,' she continued, pointing to the chairs. 'Take the weight off your feet. I won't be long.' She left reception and disappeared down the corridor towards the treatment rooms.

* * *

Rosie left the car park and walked through the double doors into the waiting room. The huddle of nurses about to go off shift stood there chatting and blocking her view, but as she glanced through a chink between them she was amazed to see Sam sitting there.

Her heart tumbled in her chest and her throat became dry. What was he doing here? His next visit would be at the out-patient clinic and that was further down the corridor on the west wing. But surely his appointment wouldn't be so soon after leaving the ward. And he'd only be in Casualty if he'd had another accident. Unless of course he'd come to see her.

It would save a lot of embarrassment if she could slip past without his seeing her. It was going to be a nightmare trying to avoid him, not that she really wanted to, but it would be for his own good, hers too in the end. After her weekend with her parents, she'd reluctantly made the decision to abide by their wishes. And she must stick to that.

They were caring parents and wanted her to be as happy with her new husband as they had been since their own arranged marriage thirty years earlier. Rosie contemplated the situation, visualising the two of them together. If they had survived and were so happy, maybe it would work for her.

But survival wasn't enough for Rosie. She wanted love. She wanted a husband and a partner, someone with whom she could share and plan for the future together.

She'd earlier thought of rebelling. Her parents wouldn't enforce the marriage. But they would be desperately hurt and disappointed if she went against their wishes. And for that reason she tried to be positive. She had agreed at least to meet the 'intended'.

The nurses were still blocking the way and a doctor joined them. Rosie could see through the little crowd that

Sam had averted his gaze to reception. That's when she slipped through into the locker room.

Once in there she took a deep breath. What was she going to do now? She couldn't just leave him out there. But she'd made the decision to slip past him and that was that. She hung up her coat and adjusted her uniform before going out to meet Sister Wilson.

'You're early, Rosie. Nothing wrong is there?' Sister Wilson asked.

'Nothing at all, Trish. The traffic was lighter than I expected.'

'Then let's get down to it. There's a lacerated finger in treatment room two. Nurse Woodbridge is treating him, but will you go in and check her out? She's one of the new first years.'

'Fine, Trish. Any majors this morning?'

'Not that you could call major,' Trish acknowledged. 'A man with chest pains first thing. We admitted him to cardiac.'

'Then I'll go and check on Woodbridge,' Rosie told her.

She was shaking physically when she left Trish Wilson and joined Nurse Woodbridge in the treatment room. As she watched the new nurse dressing the finger, Rosie's mind was still on Sam.

'That's fine,' Rosie told the nurse as the door to the treatment room opened and Sophie, the new receptionist, entered.

'There's someone outside to see you, Sister,' she whispered. 'He's been waiting since this morning. Have you a minute to spare?'

Rosie's stomach flipped. It was Sam. It must be. What would she say to him? It had to be the truth once and for all. He would surely understand.

'I'll be out when I've finished in here,' she replied, 'but tell him we're very busy, and I can only spare a couple of minutes.'

Five minutes later Rosie took a deep breath and walked down the corridor towards him. It almost broke her heart to see him. He looked so elated, and at one point she almost lost it and gave way to her emotions. But she couldn't afford to relax, to let herself go, just in case she foolishly reversed her decision.

'What are you doing here, Sam? I'll be in trouble if Sister Wilson sees me chatting,' she told him, a weak smile touching the corners of her mouth.

'But I thought you were the Sister. Surely that gives you some punch?'

'Junior Sister, Sam. But that's beside the point,' she said, her face brightening a little more. 'I was pleased to hear you'd been discharged. How are you feeling?'

'On top of the world now that I've seen you again. Don't desert me, Rosie. We haven't had a meal out yet. I thought we could arrange it now.'

Rosie became serious. 'Sorry, Sam, I can't make any arrangements. It's difficult for me to explain, here especially,' she stuttered. 'You see I'm more or less engaged to be married. My future husband and I are to meet for the first time in three months. The marriage is arranged and the date is set.

I'm sure you'll understand.'

Her explanation was garbled, her voice strangled as though she was on the verge of tears. She looked him in the eyes and tried to judge his reaction, and she thought she saw a glimmer of understanding.

'But, Rosie, you promised to see me, just the once. There's no need for your parents to know,' Sam begged, but he knew his words were futile.

'Sorry,' Rosie whispered, unable to stay around for any further response. She left hastily, not looking back to see his true reaction.

Tears were springing to her eyes as she pushed open the locker room door. That was one of the most difficult things she'd ever had to do. Their conversation had been brief and stilted, but she hadn't let down her barrier, even though she knew Sam was desperate to make some sort of arrangement with her.

Her throat tightened even more. At all costs she must control her emotions.

She didn't wanted Sister Wilson seeing her in this state.

She took out her handkerchief and blew her nose. That was better. After splashing her face with water and taking a deep breath, she returned to the treatment room.

Once her shift was complete it was late evening, and she was desperate to get back to the house and unwind. It had started to rain and the wind splattered raindrops on the Casualty Department windows. She dashed across the car park, hurriedly opened the car door and slipped inside.

She sighed. What was happening to her? She was going through agony and for what? To suit four people, her parents and their two friends, two people she didn't even know. Her parents had been in England since they married and they'd kept in touch with their friends. Between them they'd obviously thought it would be an ideal arrangement for Rosie and Imran to marry.

Imran was an only child, apparently very intelligent and revered by his parents. He sounded a real egghead from what her father had said, and he was probably spoilt by the way his parents doted on him. But she was being unkind. Her parents doted on her, didn't they? And who was to say 'the egghead' was in agreement with the arranged marriage?

★   ★   ★

Sam was stunned. He couldn't believe it. He thought he and Rosie had something going, that there was a spark between them. And surely she couldn't love someone she'd never met. But what was he thinking? He was in a similar position himself, but he had tried to stall things.

He'd come over to England eight years ago to embark upon his university course in London. And afterwards the job in Leeds cropped up, and he insisted he needed to complete his

83

education. Deep down he wanted to be free, free to choose his own partner, but he knew in the end he would not go against his father's wishes.

Dejected, he turned, left the waiting room and struggled to move outside into the fresh air. There was one thing for certain. Although he was aware of his own destiny, that could be put on hold. He could avoid returning home by convincing his mother he needed more time.

He shook his head as though to clear his mind. He was in a real dilemma. On the one hand he knew, as Rosie did, that they had no future together, yet on the other he didn't care whether she was promised or not, he was determined to win her back whatever it took.

He wandered aimlessly for a little while, stopping every few yards to lean on his crutches for relief. Eventually he set off wearily towards the bus stop. He couldn't be bothered to ring a taxi. But it was almost three o'clock, and a nearby school was spilling out its pupils, mostly teenagers, who were jostling about, play-fighting at the bus stop and almost knocking Sam down.

When he reached his flat he was practically soaked to the skin and desperately tired. He slipped off his jacket and lay on the sofa, exhausted after his struggle to the hospital and back. He was depressed too after hearing Rosie's revelation, but he was all the more determined to think of a plan, some way to get in touch with her.

★   ★   ★

Back at the house, Rosie told Katie about Sam's visit to Casualty. 'It seems such a shame you had to cut him off when he'd waited since morning,' Katie said.

'But what could I do?'

'You must admit it was a bit over the top, telling him something as important as that in the Casualty waiting room.'

'It was. But what was the alternative? Should I have asked him to wait until my shift was over to tell him in a more leisurely manner that my marriage had been arranged, that there was no way I could possibly see him again? He had to know, Katie. It was for the best. I didn't want to lead him on,' Rosie explained.

'I realise that, Rosie but couldn't you have arranged to meet him one evening to break the news more gently. And how are you going to be able to cope meeting the 'intended' when you're obviously besotted with Sam? The situation certainly doesn't lend itself to a happy marriage, not when you have someone else on your mind.' Katie paused momentarily. 'Why not talk it over with your parents?'

'First of all I'm not besotted. How could you say that?'

'I think you're kidding yourself.'

'Whatever,' Rosie said sullenly. 'And as for telling my parents, I don't want to jump the gun, Katie. Maybe Sam wants a friendship, nothing more. I can't assume he wants a serious relationship. If I take it for granted that Sam and I have something going and tell Mum and Dad about him, I could be totally wrong.'

'Then talk to Sam first. Tell him you'd like to be friends and see what he has to say. There's no harm in doing that. He knows the score about arranged marriages.'

'But what if he refuses to see me?' Rosie replied, her face a mask of anxiety.

'Then that's your answer. If he refuses to see you, he's not really interested.'

'You're right. It was rude of me to cut him off like that. But I was desperate. I didn't know what to do.' Rosie lay back on the sofa. Her face eased into a tentative half smile. Her mind was full of questions, but somehow she felt her discussion with Katie and the advice she'd been given had somehow eased the situation.

She slipped an arm through Katie's. 'Thanks for thinking it through with me. I'll do as you suggest. I'll ring him right now.'

★   ★   ★

Sheer exhaustion had set in after the day's events. Sam was asleep within minutes, and the next thing he knew the telephone was ringing. He tried to rouse himself, wondering for a moment where he was, and then he realised he was back at the flat asleep on the sofa.

He lifted himself up and leant across to the coffee table where he'd left the phone. Just as his fingers reached out and touched it, the ringing stopped. It might not have been important. Maybe they'd ring again.

But now it was time he made something to eat. Sister Gill had been right when she said he needed someone to look after him. He'd been stubborn as usual and now he was suffering the consequences. The two reasons he'd had for wanting to be out of hospital were unimportant now, the first to allow him to take Rosie out to dinner and the second to enable him to get back to work. Neither had worked out, so he may as well have stayed in there.

He opened the fridge and took out a piece of fillet steak. That was easy enough to cook. He opened the freezer and took out a bag of fries, spreading some on a baking tray. But he was about to turn on the oven when the phone started to ring again. He collected his crutches and swung into action.

Picking up the phone, he said, 'Hello.'

There was a pause and then he heard her voice, 'Sam. It's me, Rosie.'

He could hardly believe his ears. 'Rosie, where are you?'

'I'm at home and I'm sorry I was so abrupt with you this afternoon, but after the weekend with my parents I thought I'd come to a decision to do as they asked. And I had to try being strong for their sake.'

'I know, Rosie. Believe me, I do

understand. But please come and see me,' he begged.

'Tomorrow, Sam. I'll come tomorrow.'

'We'll talk it through, Rosie, nothing more,' he promised.

'I'll call in after my shift. I finish at five.'

'I can't wait to see you,' he concluded. 'And there'll be no pressure.'

Sam replaced the receiver and smiled to himself. He was going to see Rosie tomorrow and he couldn't wait.

He reflected on the time she'd called in the ward to see him. He'd caught his breath at the very vision of her. She was a strikingly beautiful woman. He was so taken aback he couldn't stop himself from staring at her delicate oval face.

He couldn't take his eyes off her. And there was a kind of sweetness about her, an innocence which intrigued him. It was so refreshing in comparison with the over-confidence of many of the young women he'd met at university.

Some tended to be wildly outspoken, and lacked that gentleness.

He pulled his thoughts together. Should he tell her about his own circumstances? Not that he had any intentions of succumbing to his mother's wishes, not yet at any rate. But he decided against broaching the subject. Why complicate things? He'd give her the chance to let off steam, to speak her mind. She deserved that after everything she'd gone through.

Perhaps he could tell her about his own circumstances at some later date, depending upon how things went. One step at a time, that was the way to tackle this one. And once everything was out in the open it would be decision time.

5

It was early evening when Sam's telephone rang again. It was Jeremy Brownwell. 'The Ritchie case, Sam. One or two problems have cropped up. Have you given it any thought?'

'The Ritchie case, Jeremy? I don't have it to hand. I believe I left it in the office,' Sam replied.

'But it was one of the files I handed over to you the day before the accident,' Brownwell insisted.

'Give me a minute and I'll check the contents again. I'm certain Ritchie isn't amongst them. I've made a start with three of them,' Sam pointed out as he struggled to the other side of the room.

He put down the receiver and picked up his briefcase, sliding the contents carefully on to the table and looking at each heading before picking up the receiver again. 'There are five cases here,' he said, 'but Ritchie's isn't one of them.'

'But I'm certain I gave you all six cases,' Jeremy insisted. 'And you'd already made a start on the Ritchie case the previous day if you recall.'

'Yes, I do. but I didn't think it was with me. Are you sure I didn't leave it in the office?'

'We've scoured the place.' Brownwell paused. 'Does that mean what I think it means, Sam, that it's either disappeared from the briefcase, or someone's taken it?'

'That's the only solution. But why would someone take it? And surely there's no reason it needs urgent attention.'

'Initially it seemed a straightforward case, a mere dispute between neighbours. Our client, Ritchie claims that his neighbour's lottery win was a shared gamble, that the five million should be split equally. But now the witness statements forwarded by Ritchie to support his claim are missing and the claim is unsubstantial. Not only that, an anonymous caller has come up with more information.

'Apparently the statements are false. My clerk, Jack, has tried to check out the source of the statements. The witnesses are husband and wife, but it seems they're non-existent. There's no-one of that name at the address we were given. And the tenants at the house say they've never heard of the couple. Meanwhile our client, Ritchie, is trying to convince us that, whilst the two statements are genuine, both witnesses have left the country. According to him they've bought a property in Spain.'

'I recall the case, Jeremy, and I had made a start. That's fair enough if they've moved to Spain. But why can't we contact them there?'

'He tells us they seem to have moved house again, and he's not in touch any longer. We could try to trace them if only we had the file. It contains additional information.'

'Don't we have photocopies, Jeremy?'

'We should have but Donna either forgot to copy them or she's misplaced them. It's all so frustrating.'

'It seems to me his claim is invalid if he can't find the witnesses, despite our having had sight of the hand-written statements earlier. They're not available now, and even if they were, we've got to remain suspicious if it's been claimed they're false.' Sam sighed deeply. 'I'd better do a spot of detective work and try to trace what happened to my briefcase before Sister Gill retrieved it. Once the notes come to hand we can pursue the case further.'

'But are you sure you can manage, Sam?'

'I'll be fine,' Sam reassured him.

'We don't want you doing anything to make that leg worse. We need you back in the office as soon as possible. Can you manage to start the ball rolling over the telephone?'

'That's what I had in mind,' Sam was quick to stress. After his outing today, he'd no intention of straining his leg again when he'd earlier convinced himself he must take it easy. He realised he'd aggravated the leg by being foolish. But he had an excuse for that after being hit with Rosie's news at the hospital.

'If you do find leg-work is needed, that's where I come in, or Jack of course. Keep in touch, Sam.'

'Don't worry, I'm not going to do anything I'll regret. But I'll start my phone calls right now. I'll fill you in on what happens, Jeremy.'

No sooner had he replaced the receiver on the hook than he picked it up again and dialled the orthopaedic ward at the hospital.

'Is Sister Gill available?' he asked.

'Sister Gill,' came the reply. 'Can I help you?'

'It's Samir Azam, Sister. Sorry to bother you, but could you give me the name of the person who brought my briefcase from Casualty?'

'It was Joe Miller, one of the porters.

But why do you need to know? Is anything wrong, Sam?'

'Well, yes. I really want to know who handled it after the accident. Something is missing from it, a very important file containing confidential information. I suppose the briefcase could have come open and the document could have dropped out.'

'I suppose so. But surely someone at the scene of the accident would have picked it up.'

'That's exactly what I thought,' Sam replied.

'It is rather alarming. What would anyone want with a file of notes?' she asked, pausing momentarily. 'I can certainly vouch for Joe's honesty. He's been with us for as long as I can remember. And I've been here a considerable number of years.'

'I'm sure you can vouch for Joe, Sister. I'm not blaming anyone. Thanks, I'll get on to Joe and find out who passed it on to him.'

'Good idea. We can do without any

sort of scandal at the hospital.'

'I agree. And I'd be most grateful if you'd keep this strictly to yourself, for the time being at any rate.'

'My lips are sealed,' she promised. 'Now then, Sam. How are you feeling? Are they looking after you back there?'

He had hoped she wouldn't ask him that. 'I'm fine, couldn't be better,' he replied avoiding answering her question directly.

'Good. I'm glad to hear it.'

'I'll let you know the outcome, Sister. Thanks for your help.'

There was nothing more Sam could do. It was getting late now and he'd no intention of ringing Casualty at that time of night to ask if Joe was on duty. But perhaps that's where Jeremy could come in. He'd ask him to talk to Joe and find out who'd handed the case to him.

After that maybe he could pick up the threads himself the following week after he'd seen Mr Rae and been given permission to go back to work. He liked to see things through to their conclusion, although he realised he needed Jeremy's help to get to know exactly who had handled his briefcase.

* * *

Rosie had surprised herself. What would her parents say if they knew she'd contacted Sam? But there was no reason why they should find out, and it didn't have to be a serious relationship. They could be good friends, nothing more. It was a pity she hadn't thought about that when she'd been so abrupt with Sam. All he'd wanted was for them to have a meal together.

The day seemed to drag and when, at five o'clock, her shift was complete, she hastily tidied herself up and left for Sam's place. On the way there she asked herself several times if this was what she should be doing, but her answer always ended in the affirmative. Why should she isolate herself? He was an ex-patient and she'd merely struck up a friendship with him.

She rang the bell and spoke to him on the intercom before going upstairs to his flat. And there he was, waiting at the door for her, carefully balancing on his crutches.

'Delighted you could make it, Rosie. As I said I haven't had the chance to thank you for saving my life.' He chuckled.

'You're doing it again,' she replied, laughing at the repeated comment. But his little joke eased them through any embarrassment in meeting up again after her announcement the previous day.

'Do come in, Rosie,' he urged and she followed him through into the lounge.

'I must say this is very impressive,' she said as she looked around and saw the size of the room. 'I like the décor.'

'It was already furnished when I took it. It's not what I would have chosen, but I must say I'm pleased with it.' He pointed to one of the sofas. 'Do sit down,' he said, 'and excuse the untidiness.'

'Don't worry about that, Sam. Katie and I are always having to tidy round, especially if someone's coming to visit.'

'Katie? Is she your flatmate?' Sam asked her.

'It's not a flat, it's a small terraced house. Katie shares with me. But of course I don't know what'll happen when I leave. I don't think she'll be able to afford to keep it on.'

She avoided eye contact, realising that, in a circumspect way, she was touching upon that dreaded subject, the arranged marriage. But she couldn't let him think things had changed drastically.

It was as though he realised her embarrassment, and he smiled but failed to comment which made it easier for her.

She looked through into the kitchen and saw the sink was full of crockery.

'Is anyone looking after you, Sam?' she asked, a concerned frown sketching her face. 'You know you're not supposed to be discharged without someone to look after you.'

'I'd hoped you wouldn't mention it. I don't want it to go back to Sister Gill,' he stressed, 'but no. I'm managing on my own.'

'Shame on you. You must have told a few porkies when you were discharged.' Rosie shook her head and tutted.

'Not really. I just told Sister that my landlady lived down below. She made her own assumptions.'

'Then I hope you don't mind if I slip into the kitchen and do the washing up. I can't bear to see a sink full of crockery, not that I'm so house-proud, but I'm sure every little helps.'

'Oh,' he gasped, 'I couldn't let you do that. I didn't expect you to come and start doing household chores,' he added, pulling himself to his feet.

'But I'll feel satisfied if I do something for you, so just you sit there and talk whilst I get on with it,' she urged. 'I'll have it all done and put away in no time.'

Sam sat down again on the sofa and relaxed. 'I'm back at the hospital to see Mr Rae again next week. I can't wait to be given the go ahead to go back to work,' he told her.

'How are you going to get there, to work, I mean?' Rosie asked him.

'They'll send a car for me and bring me back home. I'll probably get more rest there than I get at home. They'll only let me do what they think fit.'

'I should think so, too,' she said as she dried the crockery and placed it on the work-top. 'Now where do these go? Don't get up. Just tell me and I'll do it.'

But Sam was already standing up and reaching for the kitchen door without using his crutches. 'Just up there in the top cupboard' He let go of the door and pointed.

'Careful, Sam. Don't slip on the floor. It might be wet with drips from the washing up,' she claimed.

'I'm fine, Rosie. Don't worry,' he assured her, but no sooner had the words left his lips than he lurched forward.

Rosie's reactions were quick. She opened her arms and caught him, almost overbalancing herself with the effort. But he was heavy and he started to slip through her arms.

'Sorry,' he kept on repeating as he grabbed the kitchen work-top with one hand and clung to her with the other.

He balanced himself and relaxed slightly, looking into her eyes. Their faces were mere centimetres apart, and she knew what he was about to do. He kissed her gently on the lips and then drew himself away, clinging on to the kitchen top with both hands now.

'That was for saving me, nothing more,' he urged, the light dancing in his laughing eyes. 'Sorry, I just couldn't help myself.'

They both started to laugh. 'Excuses, excuses,' Rosie said to cover her embarrassment. She made sure he was clinging on to the work-top before she walked through into the lounge, picked up the crutches and handed them to him. 'Now do exactly as you're told and sit down, will you?'

'Right you are, madam,' he said as he placed his arms on the crutches and foolishly gave a salute, almost falling once more.

Rosie felt comfortable with Sam and she enjoyed his humour. Surely she was allowed to meet people and gather some experience before she was forced to settle down and marry someone she didn't even know?

Once the kitchen chores were through she went back into the lounge and sat down next to Sam.

'I suppose I've been trying to avoid touching on the subject of my impending marriage, but it's so difficult when it's to someone I've never met. It seems like a fantasy.'

'I'm sure it does, Rosie. What I can't understand is that you've never met the man you're marrying. Why is that?'

'He's apparently been out of the country for some time. As far as I'm concerned he can stay away as long as he wishes. I'm in no hurry.'

Sam smiled. 'OK, Rosie. Now we've mulled that one over, shall we put it aside for now? Believe me, I'm not expecting a serious relationship because I know that's not possible, but do let's stay friends,' he pleaded.

'Yes, friends,' she repeated. 'That suits me.'

'It's good this friendship thing,' he said, taking her hand in his and smiling, a smug look on his face. 'Now about that meal? Can you manage tomorrow night?' he enquired.

'I can't manage this week at all. I'm on late shift.'

'So you are. I should have remembered that from yesterday. How about next Tuesday? It's my check-up at the hospital Monday. Is Tuesday OK?'

'You'll never let up until I agree, will you? Tuesday's fine. Would you like me to pick you up from the flat?'

'That's better still,' he agreed. 'I can't believe my luck. Not only have I found a new friend but I have a chauffeur too.'

'I shall expect you to reciprocate when you're back on your feet,' she joked.

'With the promise of yet another meal out, I agree,' he replied, clapping his hands and almost losing his balance again. 'How about Italian?'

'You're on,' she echoed. 'Shall we say seven o'clock?'

'That'll be great,' he said. 'I'll look forward to it.'

'I must be going now, Sam. It's getting late and I've one or two jobs to do before I get off to bed.' Rosie stood up ready to leave. She took hold of Sam's hand. 'You stay there. I can see myself out. I'll see you next week,' she concluded and she leaned forward and gave him a peck on the cheek before leaving the apartment.

★   ★   ★

It was dark outside and the night air was cool when she left the building. She hurried towards her car which was parked across the road and, once inside, she pressed the lock button for safety, and started up the ignition.

It was then she noticed a piece of paper underneath one of the wind-screen wipers. Surely it couldn't be a parking ticket. She looked around. There was no-one about. She unlocked the door and stepped outside, looking up for a sign to make sure it wasn't a 'no-parking' area.

She collected the slip of paper and stepped back into the car, quickly locking the door again. It was strange how nervous she'd become since the incident at the reservoir and the caller at her house.

She switched on the light above her and looked at the folded sheet of paper. It was no parking ticket, nor was it anything official. It was a sheet of lined paper torn from a notebook. She opened it up and read it:

I know all about your little affair. Watch your back!

Her heart started to thump aggressively in her chest, and she looked around through the car windows wondering if there might be someone lurking. She checked the door once more and set off for home.

Who knew about Sam other than Katie? Of course she'd told Abby, Emma and Rick. But it wouldn't be any of those three.

Surely it couldn't be anything to do with her parents or any of the community back at home in Birmingham? The only relative living in England was Uncle Khalid. He was elderly and he wasn't the type to do such a thing himself, although he was from the old school of thinking, and he did feel strongly about arranged marriages. He believed that those betrothed during childhood were destined to be together.

None of it made any sense to Rosie. And although she was scared, she didn't intend breaking off her friendship with Sam. That's all it was, friendship.

She parked the car and walked up the garden path towards the front door. It was then she thought she heard a scrunching sound as though someone was walking down the gravel drive where she'd left the car. She didn't look back. Hastily she took out her key and unlocked the door, slamming it quickly behind her. She turned the key in the lock.

Now she was being paranoid. It was probably all in her mind.

'Are you in, Katie?' she called out.

'I'm in the bedroom,' Katie replied. 'I'm glad you're back. I've had a phone message for you. It was a man. He sounded foreign. He asked me to tell you he'd be in touch. I asked his name but by that time he'd replaced the receiver. He sounded friendly enough.'

'That's strange. I wonder who it could be.' She was puzzled. There were so many things going on. But perhaps none of the recent incidents were connected. She hoped not.

All the same she was perturbed.

Everything seemed to be happening at once, and all since Sam's accident. First the stalking, then the mysterious caller, tonight the note and now the anonymous telephone call. What had she done to deserve this? Maybe when she saw Sam again, she'd confide in him.

6

Jeremy Brownwell swung open the doors to Casualty in search of Joe Miller. The girl on reception told him she'd try to catch him when he came back from the wards. It was twenty minutes later when Jeremy had the chance to talk to him.

'I gather you recently handed a briefcase over to Sister Gill on the orthopaedic ward. We have it now, but I need to trace its whereabouts from the time it went missing. How did it come into your possession?'

'I think it was Dr Holgate who found it in Casualty. Sister Wilson asked me to take it down to the orthopaedic ward. She told me they knew who it belonged to,' Joe replied. 'There's nothing wrong is there?'

'Something's gone missing from the briefcase and we're trying to trace it.'

'It's nothing to do with me. I didn't even open the case,' he declared, pulling his small frame upright and folding his arms. 'And I'm not a thief. What money I have, I've earned honestly,' he stressed in defence.

'Don't worry, Joe. It wasn't money. It was a file containing documents. I'm sure I can eliminate you from the frame. But is Dr Holgate on duty this morning? If so, I'd like a word with him.'

Joe pointed down the corridor. 'He's just gone into treatment room three. Give him a couple of minutes and then I'll go along and tell him you're here.'

'Thanks, Joe. I need to get to the bottom of this as soon as possible.'

'If you'll take a seat in the waiting room, I'll ask him to see you when he's free.'

It was ten more minutes before Dr Holgate came down to the waiting room.

'I haven't much time to spare,' he urged. 'You can see the crowd we have here this morning,' he added with a faint smile, 'but Joe tells me you're enquiring about the briefcase we had in Casualty last week. I looked inside to see who it belonged to. It came in with the patient. The ambulance drivers must have picked it up and left it in one of the treatment rooms, but it was a couple of days before it was found.

'I don't know which ambulance crew brought it in, but if you get on to them they'll no doubt check it out.' The doctor smiled. 'It's a strange request asking who picked up the briefcase, but I suppose you have your reasons.'

'That's right, sir. Thanks for your help.' Jeremy replied, not wishing to go through the information again. When the doctor returned to the treatment rooms Jeremy turned to Joe.

'Which ambulance station would they be from, Joe?'

'The one in Browgate. I'm sure they'll be able to help, as long as you know the exact time of the accident.'

'You've been most helpful. Thank

you very much, Joe.' Jeremy turned to leave.

'I hope you get to the bottom of it, Mr Brownwell. It's a funny carry on, pinching a file of papers.' Shaking his head and frowning, Joe walked down the corridor towards the porters' day room.

Jeremy collected his car from the car park and set off towards Browgate. The traffic was busy but it didn't take him long to reach the station. One of the officers was on reception as he entered the building.

'Can I help you, sir?' he asked.

'I hope so,' Jeremy answered slipping a business card from his pocket and placing it on the desk. The man looked over the top of his glasses and peered at it.

'Well then, Mr Brownwell. What can we do for you?'

'It's about a road accident in the city last week, on the twenty-fourth to be exact in Bank Street. I'd say it happened about seven fifteen in the morning. A colleague of mine was knocked down by a car. I need to know who attended the accident.'

'Is there some reason why you need that information, sir? Is it important?'

'It is. The victim had a briefcase with him. I'd like to know who collected it.'

'Surely it went with the victim,' the officer said, a puzzled look on his face. 'Is it missing or something?'

'The briefcase isn't, but certain items are missing from it and I thought one of the crew might let me know if anyone looked inside to check the victim's address or something like that.'

'I see,' the officer mumbled. He clicked on the mouse and peered at the screen in front of him. 'The accident in Bank Street you say?'

'Yes, that's right.'

'It was Kev O'Brien and Alan Bridger. Alan's in this morning. I'll call him down,' the officer replied switching on the intercom and delivering a message.

A couple of minutes later a uniformed ambulance attendant came whistling towards them and reported to the desk. 'You wanted me?' he said. The officer filled him in about the missing documents.

'The Bank Street accident, yes I remember,' he repeated after listening to the officer on reception.

'That's right,' Jeremy replied. 'It's about the briefcase you took to Casualty with Sam Azam. Do you recall anyone opening it — to check the victim's address for instance?'

'As far as I know it wasn't touched before we collected it. But there was a fair old crowd there when we arrived. Someone could have opened it earlier. We picked it up and left it in Casualty. That bonny little dark-haired nurse was there when we arrived at the scene of the accident, Sister Khan, Rosie I think she's called. She works in Casualty. She might be able to help.' He leant with his elbows on the desk. 'If, as you say, something's missing, it could have been taken anywhere, more likely before we arrived than afterwards. But why would anyone need documents?'

'I can't divulge any information about the file, but it was confidential.'

'Sorry I can't be more helpful. But I'll have a word with Kev when he's on duty, and let you know if he noticed anything.'

Jeremy was disappointed he hadn't discovered more. If it came down to the public at large, as Alan had said, it could be anyone. And it might be someone who took the documents thinking they were valuable.

Back at the office Jeremy telephoned Sam. 'I'm no further with my enquiries, Sam,' Jeremy told him, explaining what had happened.

'Perhaps we should forget about it and start again,' Sam suggested.

'Maybe you're right but we're not in the habit of representing clients who can't be straight with us, even if they are guilty. We need to get at the exact truth to be able to act on behalf of Ritchie. But, as you say, we'll have to leave it until you return, hopefully next week. If anything crops up I'll let you know.'

'That's fine, Jeremy. And I agree with what you're saying. I couldn't defend someone who couldn't be truthful. But we'll wait and see what happens.'

Later that day Jeremy had a telephone call from Kevin O'Brien, the second of the two ambulance attendants. O'Brien seemed keen to co-operate.

'It's about the briefcase you mentioned, the one belonging to Samir Azam. Alan was right. I collected it from the pavement before we carried Mr Azam into the ambulance. Sister Khan was attending to Azam.

'Apparently she was on her way home when she saw the accident happen. I didn't think anything about it at the time. But she was carrying a large handbag, you know one of those that looks almost like a shopping bag. I seem to recall something sticking out at the top. When I think back, I must admit it looked like some sort of folder.'

'How do you know it wasn't hers?'

119

'I don't. But who attends to an accident victim with a large folder in their bag. Nurse Khan had left her car and crossed the road. Why would she bring it with her? I thought it was strange at the time, but I didn't say anything to Alan. In any case, it's obvious he didn't notice. He wouldn't have said anything anyway. I think he's sweet on the girl.'

'I see,' Brownwell replied. 'Well thanks for the information Mr O'Brien. I think I need to visit Sister Khan and find out exactly what happened.'

⋆   ⋆   ⋆

It was early afternoon when Rosie had a visit from Bronwwell's clerk, a Mr Jack Weston.

'They informed us at the ambulance station that you were on the scene when a Mr Azam was knocked down by a car a couple of weeks ago.'

'That's right,' Rosie told him, puzzled as to why she was being interviewed.

120

'I'm from his firm of solicitors and we're anxious to check the whereabouts of a briefcase from the time of the accident to the time it appeared in Casualty a couple of days later.'

'I was at the scene before the ambulance arrived. I was busy checking out the victim. I didn't notice a briefcase. What I do know is that the briefcase turned up eventually. I visited Mr Azam and he had the briefcase with him. I particularly noticed because there were papers strewn across the bed. Sorry I can't be of more help.'

'Did you stay with Mr Azam at the time of the accident and go back to the hospital with him?'

'I didn't stay, no. Once the ambulance arrived the attendants insisted they could manage. And it would have been unprofessional of me to stay. We have to be careful not to step on each other's toes. Once they arrived Mr Azam was in their care and that's when I left.' She didn't tell him she was more or less shooed away by Kevin O'Brien.

'But it seems rather strange that when the briefcase was eventually found in Casualty there was a file missing.'

'I agree, Mr Weston. But I know nothing about it.'

'This is a little delicate, Sister, but we have a witness who tells us you had a large handbag with you. They say there was a folder sticking out of the top of it. Is that true?'

'A folder in my handbag? What next?' Rosie laughed. 'That really takes the biscuit. I might have a multitude of bits and bobs in my bag but I'm not in the habit of carrying folders in it.'

'I'm only repeating what I was told.'

'By whom, may I ask?'

'I'm not at liberty to say, Sister, but thank you for your help,' he said as, shaking his head, he left the hospital.

It was Monday morning and Rosie was back on the early shift, in charge until Sister Wilson arrived after lunch. Casualty was overflowing with minor injury patients referred by their GPs after weekend accidents. But Rosie needed her morning break and, aware that during the morning Sam would be attending out-patients to see Mr Rae, she decided to pop along there and see if he was around.

'Staff Nurse Grant, I'm on coffee break until half past. I'll either be in the staff room or in out-patients. If you need me give me a call,' she urged.

She collected a cup of coffee and went along to out-patients where she searched the waiting room for Sam. But he was nowhere to be seen. She went across to reception and asked, 'Has Sam Azam been through yet?'

'I think he's gone to x-ray before he sees Mr Rae,' the clerk told her.

'Thanks, Kath. I'll see if he's still there,' she replied as she headed down the corridor and spotted him sitting outside x-ray. 'There you are, Sam.'

'Lovely to see you, Rosie.' He smiled eagerly and lifted his hand to take hers but, obviously realising where he was, he replaced it on his lap. 'I'm keeping my fingers crossed Mr Rae will let me go back to work.' He looked her up and down. 'I must say that uniform suits you.'

Rosie laughed. 'You say that every time you see me. Some people have a thing about uniforms and yet, I can't wait to get out of it and into something casual.'

The radiographer interrupted their conversation. 'Sam Azam. Come through please.'

'Pop into Casualty when you're through and tell me how you get on,' Rosie whispered.

'I'll do that,' he replied as he placed the crutches in front of him and pulled himself to his feet.

Rosie was at lunch when Sam called back at Casualty, and staff nurse sent one of the probationary nurses to let her know.

'How's it gone? You're looking smug,' she said, smiling as she sat beside him.

'Mr Rae wanted me to take another week off, but I explained the circumstances and he relented. So tomorrow

I'm back at work.'

'Up to your tricks again and getting your own way I see,' Rosie said, shaking her head.

Sam rubbed his hands gleefully. 'You must admit. It's not as though I'm going to be doing anything overly active. Just sitting at my desk in the office. Anyway, enough of that. I'm looking forward to our dinner together.'

'Me too, Sam. But do take care.' She stood up to leave. 'I must get back now. My lunch break is just about over. I'll see you tomorrow night at seven.'

Sam pushed on his crutches and stood up. 'I'll take care, don't you worry.'

The afternoon was less busy and Rosie was ready to leave by five. She'd be early for the walk that evening but she had a little shopping to do before she met up with the gang.

As she sat in the car waiting, she realised the last time she met up with her friends was the previous Friday.

Rick was first to appear. He waved

and crossed the car park towards her, opening the passenger door and sitting beside her. That familiar, unmistakable aroma filled the car and her stomach churned.

'How are you?' he asked, leaning across and giving her a peck on the cheek.

'I'm fine,' she replied. 'How's university? Has your workload increased since the promotion?'

'Just the reverse. I now have an extra two free periods,' he told her, looking up and pointing to the other side of the car park where Abby and Emma were drawing up together. 'Here are the others,' he continued as he stepped out of the car, dashed towards them and gave them both a peck on the cheek. 'Are we ready?' he asked.

Rosie took stock of the situation. The business of the stalker had been triggered off again by the scent of the aftershave Rick was wearing. But surely it couldn't be him. And then there was the business of the note on her car.

The only person who knew about Sam was Katie, and she'd been home all night. In any case, why would she want to do anything like that? Someone had obviously followed her to Sam's apartment. But who?

Back at the flat she continued to mull things over in her mind when the door opened and Katie came in. 'Hi, Rosie. Did you see the letter I left for you on the mantelpiece?'

'No, I haven't been in long, Katie,' she replied as she walked across to the fireplace and picked up the letter. The handwriting was familiar. The letter was from her mother. Rosie slipped her thumb through the flap and slit open the envelope.

She must put on a brave face when she met up with Sam. Whether to reveal the contents of her mother's letter or not was another matter. Perhaps it would be best to get the evening over with first.

After all Sam had looked forward to their meal together and it would be a shame to spoil it. The best way would be to let him down gently. Maybe she could arrange to call on him at the apartment some other time in the near future, and tell him exactly what was happening.

But that would be after she'd met up with her parents again. She needed to iron one or two things out before she made a final decision.

It was a bright evening but there was a chill in the air. Rosie decided to wear a fine woollen skirt which was flared below the hips, and a matching silk blouse beneath a suede jacket.

Still feeling depressed after reading the letter, she took a few deep breaths before she rang the bell to the flat. She settled a lively smile on her face before Sam opened the door.

'Rosie, you look gorgeous,' he whooped, taking her hands and planting a kiss on her cheek.

'Now don't you be getting too confident answering the door without your sticks,' Rose replied, laughing at his enthusiasm, hoping to keep up the bravado, even though inside she was dreading the future.

'Are you managing better with the sticks than the crutches,' she continued.

'Much better,' he told her. 'They're less cumbersome.'

She turned to cross the corridor. 'Stay there,' she ordered good-humouredly, pointing a finger at him. 'I'll bring up the lift. I don't want to be responsible for any accidents.'

'Ay, ay, Ma'am,' he replied and, when he tried to salute in response to her playful comment, his sticks clattered to the floor and he wobbled, but he managed to grab the door jamb before he fell.

Sam struggled to lock the door and he followed Rosie towards the lift. 'Now watch me. Am I being careful or not?'

'Not before time. You're a fool, Sam. And stop trying to impress me. I'll take your word for it,' she accepted as the lift door opened and they stepped inside.

It was busy at Bella Italia when they arrived.

'I'm surprised,' Rosie said. 'I thought it would have been quiet this early.'

'There's a birthday party in the conservatory,' the waiter chipped in. 'Have you booked?'

'Yes, the name's Azam,' Sam told him. 'Table for two, seven fifteen.'

'Come this way,' the waiter beckoned. 'There's a nice little table ready for you by the window.'

Rosie made sure Sam went ahead of her, and he wove his way carefully between the tables.

'Are you OK here?' the waiter asked him. 'Have you enough room? It must be tricky having to walk with sticks.'

'I'm fine,' Sam told him. 'Once I'm seated there's no problem.' And when he looked up again, the waiter had returned with the wine list and the menus.

Sam turned to Rosie. 'You will have a glass of wine, won't you?'

'Not for me, Sam. I'm careful when

I'm driving. I know I could probably drink one glass, but it's not worth risking it. Still water for me, please.'

'I respect your decision, Rosie, but do you mind if I have a glass, just to celebrate?'

'Celebrate?'

'Yes, celebrate your saving my life,' he offered, a cheeky grin touching the corners of his mouth.

'You have a fixation about me saving your life, Sam. What is it with you?'

'I mean saving my life in more ways than one. My life was boring until I met you. And now the quality has improved tremendously.'

Rosie's stomach gave a tiny lurch. If only he knew the full score. But she'd made a decision not to mention anything until after their meal together, and she was determined to stick with it.

'By the way,' Rosie said to Sam, 'I had a visit from a Mr Jack Weston yesterday afternoon. He asked me if I'd seen your briefcase.'

'Jack Weston came to see you?' Sam

shook his head in bewilderment. And then it seemed he realised the reason why. 'They're checking things out. You must be on the list.'

'On the list?'

'The list of suspects,' Sam replied calmly.

'What's it all about, Sam?' Rosie asked him, now feeling a little prickly at being labelled a suspect.

'There was a folder containing case notes. It went missing from my briefcase. They're checking out what happened to the briefcase from the time of the accident to the time when it was collected from Casualty.'

'I see. So they think someone's taken the notes.'

'They're not sure whether the case came open and the folder slipped out or if someone took the folder.'

'I was just curious as to why they were checking up. I hope you find it. Is it very important?'

'It is actually. It contains original witness testimonies,' he stressed.

'I hope they don't think I took the folder,' Rosie asserted, but Sam didn't answer her directly, and Rosie felt a frisson of annoyance.

'They don't know who took it but they have to check everyone's story. That's the only way we can get to the bottom of it.'

Rosie resented the fact that she was on the list of suspects. She and Sam were friends, weren't they? And friends usually trust one another. What sort of trust was that? And why would Sam allow Jack Weston to interview her if he knew she wasn't involved? Surely he didn't suspect her of taking the file?

It was not until the following weekend that Rosie had an opportunity to visit her parents. She stepped inside the house in trepidation, foolishly hoping that things had changed since she received her mother's letter. But they hadn't.

'Rosina, darling, it's lovely to see you. Your father and I were delighted at the good news. But you're not looking very happy.'

'But, Mum, I was surprised when I received your letter. You say that Imran is coming earlier than I expected. I'm not ready for this. I don't know if I can go through with it. I've never met him and we may not get on.'

'We're not forcing you, my lovely Rosina,' her father implored. 'But please give it a chance. It's the same for Imran. Let's see how it goes. Will you give it a try? For our sake.'

What could she say? There was no obligation. And why not meet up with Imran? She had another six weeks to put things in order. But maybe she didn't need to put anything in order.

After the conversation with Sam about the missing folder, she'd decided to cool it with him. He'd pressurised her about the meal and she'd given in.

She hadn't seen him since that evening, and the way she was feeling, she didn't intend seeing him again in a hurry. The more she thought about the calm way he'd reacted when she'd told him about Jack Weston's visit, the more annoyed she became.

But back to the idea of meeting up with Imran. If the arrangement could eventually be negated, there was no harm in going along with her parents' wishes.

'OK, you two. I'll meet up with Imran, for your sakes. But I'm not going to hand in my notice at the hospital, not until we've made a definite decision. When will he be here?'

'That's wonderful, Rosina. But we're not sure when he'll be here. All we know is that it'll be earlier than we thought. And I'm sure you'll like him. According to Shazia he's very intelligent and very caring.'

'Just one thing, Mother,' Rosie said. 'You told me you'd already arranged the wedding. Please cancel it until we've met and made a decision.'

'There are no definite arrangements yet, Rosina, just dates when the wedding could take place. Don't worry.

135

We'll abide by your wishes, darling.'

It seemed they were still hoping the relationship would be successful. But at least Rosie felt she was being given some breathing space, and the opportunity to decide for herself whether or not the arrangement would work. Best of all she was still a free spirit.

7

Rosie felt as though a weight had been lifted from her shoulders. The fact that her parents had agreed to allow the couple to make their own decisions had given her new hope. She might like Imran after all. But one thing she did know, she couldn't possibly fall in love with him. Until recently that had been reserved for someone else.

But here she was, running ahead of herself. All the time she was involved with Sam she'd never once thought about a permanent relationship. Actually she didn't really know all that much about him. But enough of Sam. He was in the past, and the future now beckoned.

It was a few days later when Sam telephoned her at the house and asked if she'd go along to the cinema with him. They were showing *Chicago* locally and since she hadn't seen it the first time around, Sam asked if she'd like to go. He'd obviously remembered that she was a fan of the two main stars in the cast.

'Sorry, Sam. I can't make it.'

'How about tomorrow?'

'Nor tomorrow. I think you know why.'

'But, Rosie, has something happened for you to push me out?'

'Let's say I wasn't too excited at being interviewed as a suspect.'

'I'm sorry, Rosie. The word suspect was a rather unfortunate choice. I didn't mean it that way. And it wasn't my doing. It was my colleagues who were trying to speak to anyone who might know something,' he stressed. 'And in any case, the folder turned up in the post yesterday. The package contained a Leeds post mark. It's a mystery but at least we have it back.'

'So you don't need to worry about that any longer. I suppose you think I posted it back,' Rosie told him.

'You're being silly now, Rosie. Come on. Call it a truce. Sorry about any misunderstanding.'

'But it's not just that, Sam. Arrangements have been made for me to meet up with my future husband. I can't see you again, Sam, sorry,' she concluded, replacing the receiver on the hook.

There, she'd done it. She needn't worry about Sam any longer. Whatever their relationship, it was over, for good.

Rosie reached the reservoir car park in good time. It was a bright fresh morning but there was no-one around, and the only car in the car park was a solitary dark green one, a rather battered old Jaguar. There didn't appear to be anyone in it and Rosie guessed it belonged to one of the old gentlemen who regularly walked their dogs along the reservoir path.

Within minutes Abby appeared followed by Emma and Rick who arrived together in one car. Rosie was puzzled. They usually travelled in separate cars. It must be some special arrangement.

'Hi there,' Rosie called out as the three of them walked towards her. 'I'm on late shift this week, so hopefully I'll make the morning stints.'

'Great,' Abby replied. 'We're back to our little team once more.'

They set off at a stiff pace, Rick and Emma ahead and Abby behind with Rosie.

'By the way, Rosie, I wonder what happened to the stalker. We never found out why he picked on you. Did you ever hear anything more from the police after you reported him?'

'Not a word. Nor did the warden have anything to report when I met him in the car park last week.'

'That was very strange,' Abby commented. 'Usually when there's someone like that around there's a spate of attacks or, at least, sightings.'

'I know, but of course I've not been here on my own since that evening, so he hadn't had the chance to follow me again.'

'Rick and Emma seem to be getting

rather chummy,' Abby whispered.

'I wouldn't know, Abby, I missed the mornings last week, but I was surprised they came together today.'

'I hope they have something going,' Abby continued. 'They're good together. And Rick is so caring — like the way he begged you not to walk alone again.'

'I know,' Rosie replied, now feeling guilty that she'd even suspected that Rick could be the stalker.

When Rosie returned to the house, Katie had left for the office. It was her turn to do the washing and before she left for the hospital she managed to visit the launderette and do some of the ironing afterwards. Katie would complete the rest when she returned from work in the evening.

The roads seemed busier than usual. There was a trickling queue of traffic when she cut into the main road and gradually the queue came to a standstill. She was glad she hadn't left it until the last minute to leave for work, otherwise she would have been late for her shift.

She waited patiently, thinking about her forthcoming meeting with Imran. Three weeks and they would meet. Her stomach churned. She didn't want to face that situation but she knew she'd promised her parents. And she must stick to that promise.

Eventually the traffic started to move, slowly at first and then it began to clear. Maybe there'd been an accident. But there seemed to be no evidence. She hadn't heard the sound of police or ambulance sirens.

Just as she was thinking it was one of those inexplicable situations where the traffic has slowed down seemingly for no apparent reason, she spotted an old car in a lay-by. She recognised it as the old green Jaguar she'd seen in the car park earlier that morning.

It was definitely the same car. It had a rusty roof-rack on top. But that wasn't the only thing that surprised her. There at the front of the car, standing beneath an open bonnet was the ambulance attendant Kevin O'Brien, the one who'd been rude to her on the day of Sam's accident.

How strange, she thought. She wouldn't have taken the car to belong to him. It was more the sort of car she'd earlier believed would belong to an old person. But there you go. There's no accounting for taste.

She drove past and she was still in good time when she arrived at the hospital. Sister Wilson was completing her duty and she seemed to be in a good mood. Casualty was quiet when Rosie left the locker room.

'We've had a fair old night,' Sister Wilson told her. 'You've missed it all.'

'Missed it all?'

'There was a football match in the city last night. A fight broke out amongst the fans and, of course, night staff took the brunt of it. But we continued this morning. There were dozens of them, black eyes, cuts and bruises, you name it, we had the full range. Most of them were minor injuries but we had a couple of boys taken into orthopaedics, one with a broken leg and the other with a torn knee cartilage.'

'Then it's kept you busy. At least the time passes quickly when that happens.'

'You can say that again, Rosie. I'm exhausted. I'll be glad to get into bed. Hope you have a quieter day, love. I'll see you tomorrow.'

There was some respite for Rosie and her team during the later part of the afternoon, but just as they began to relax there was a road accident and several ambulances had to be called to bring in the injured. A coach-load of school children had been returning from a trip when the coach had skidded and overturned. None of the children were seriously injured but most had bruising and lacerations, one or two had head injuries.

By nine o'clock things were slowing down. Most of the children had been seen. The final ambulance arrived just before Rosie went off duty at ten. And who should be the attendants but the two who'd arrived on the scene when Sam had been knocked down, Alan the cheerful one and Kevin the arrogant one she'd seen earlier in the day with his broken-down Jaguar.

'Hello, love,' Alan said. 'Haven't seen you for ages. Been on holiday, have you?'

'No, I haven't been on holiday yet. You just haven't been lucky enough to catch me,' she joked.

Kevin scowled but refrained from commenting.

'We have an elderly lady here, Rosie. She seems to have turned on a gas tap and not lit it. I don't think she inhaled much. A neighbour called — shortly after it happened we think. He rang for us and we found the woman slumped by the door. I think she must have passed out before she had the chance to light it. It could have been a stroke.'

'Bring her into cubicle two, Alan.' Rosie turned to the staff nurse. 'Dr Holgate's going to be really chuffed.

He's just gone for his break. Would you call him back, Viv?'

Alan turned to his colleague. 'Cubicle two, Kev,' he repeated and the two disappeared back into the ambulance.

Rosie flipped a clean sheet on to the trolley in cubicle two and prepared to receive the elderly woman. Alan and Kevin appeared and brought the woman through on a stretcher.

Rosie stepped back to let them pass and as she did so Kevin pushed his way past her.

She shrank back. That distinctive aroma of aftershave drifted towards her. And then everything fell into place.

First of all seeing that car in the car park this morning, and now this. Was it him? Was Kevin O'Brien the stalker?

★   ★   ★

Sam had his suspicions about the two witnesses after the anonymous phone call when the caller had stated that the couple hadn't been in England for some considerable time. And despite thorough checks and various leads, the couple could not be contacted.

'You do realise, Mr Ritchie, that unless we are able to contact the witnesses, we have no solid proof that they actually exist.'

'But you were quite willing to accept the statements before the file went missing. Why the change of mind?'

'It's not as simple as that. We had a phone call from a man who insisted that the statements were fake, that the couple had not been in England for at least two years. And despite that, when the matter goes to court we shall need to contact the witnesses, we shall need an address.'

'But why should you believe some idiot prankster over me?'

'This is a very serious matter, Mr Ritchie. If the police got wind of this and could prove that the couple did not complete those statements, that in fact their names had been used falsely, someone would be liable to imprisonment for forgery.'

'Anyone would think I'd written the statements myself the way they are talking.'

'But that's just it. Witness statements need to be signed here in the office, or failing that, we need to have contact with the people themselves.'

'I've already told you I've no idea where they've moved to. All I know is that it's somewhere in Spain.'

'Then I suggest you continue your efforts to contact the couple. We could continue on your behalf but that seems futile. And it would only cost you more money. You could try another firm of solicitors. I'm sorry, Mr Ritchie, we can't represent you when the evidence is so flimsy.'

'He won't get away with this,' Ritchie vowed as he stood up to collect the file.

'How do you mean?' Sam said, taking the file from him. 'You obviously know the name of the man who called the office. I suggest you go back and sort it out with him.' He stood up to see Ritchie out. 'If you'd like us to continue on your behalf, come back with the information about your two friends. Otherwise I'll send our account for the work done so far, and when it's paid I'll return this,' he declared, waving the file in the air.

Ritchie looked back and glared. 'You've got it in for me, haven't you?' he called out as he left the office. 'Why did you have to take over? What was wrong with the other guy?'

'It would have been the same decision whoever represented you. Goodbye, Mr Ritchie,' Sam said and he closed the door behind him.

Sam couldn't help but wonder who had taken the folder of case notes from his briefcase. Had they really dropped out or had someone taken a look inside and decided to keep the folder.

It seemed rather strange that whoever took them knew of the activities of Ritchie, but he supposed it could have been co-incidental. Either that or someone had followed him.

But he would have known had

someone been following him. He was observant. That sort of thing never escaped him, although he did have his father's words on his mind when the accident happened.

It looked as though he and Ritchie had parted company, especially after Sam had refused to accept such tenuous evidence. But it was still a mystery as to who had taken the case notes, and how that person had managed to hide the folder away. However, it seemed of little significance now that the case was in all probability closed.

8

Kevin O'Brien began to reflect on the day of the incident. It had been late when he'd finished his duty and, once at the house, he went upstairs, took off his uniform, and slipped on a pair of jeans and a sweatshirt. Back downstairs, he picked up a file from the table and flicked through the contents. He'd checked the pockets of the accident victim to establish a name. The card had read, *Samir Azam, Solicitor*, and the company he worked for was *Bickerdyke & Wagstaff*.

The name triggered off a vague recollection in his mind. It sounded familiar. And then it came to him. Wasn't Azam the guy his friend, Brian Ritchie, had set on to make a claim on his neighbour's lottery winnings? Of course, that was it. Kevin couldn't be more certain. It was an unusual name, one he wouldn't easily forget.

Kevin and Brian had been friends for years, until Ritchie tried to claim a half share of Gary Temple's five million pounds. Ritchie had then discarded Kevin, apparently assuming he wouldn't need friends once he got his hands on the money. Kevin hadn't approved of Ritchie's scam, but he hadn't made any noises, although he wasn't sure exactly how Ritchie intended to prove his entitlement.

But Kevin, an ambulance driver earning a mere pittance was bitter at Ritchie's attitude. Surely if the scam went through and Ritchie managed to get his hands on the two-and-a-half million he claimed to be rightfully his, Kevin would have qualified for some small token — in recognition of their friendship.

He collected Azam's briefcase from the pavement and placed it inside the ambulance next to the unconscious victim. It was only when he'd settled the patient, and when his partner, Alan was driving to the hospital, that he could afford to have a sneaky look. He was curious.

Inside was the file headed Ritchie, and as he suspected it, Brian Ritchie. How fortuitous to come across the briefcase and the notes. He couldn't believe it. Kevin knew the contents of the briefcase would be strictly confidential but there was no harm in looking through them.

He opened the file and flicked the pages over. Ritchie had produced witness statements from a married couple, whom he claimed had been present when the agreement to share the lottery ticket with Gary Temple had been made. Kevin gasped and shook his head. So that was how he'd planned to get his hands on the money?

Kevin knew the witnesses had been in Spain for the past year and he was certain they hadn't been back to England since then, simply because they'd left behind a heap of debts. They couldn't afford to come back and face their creditors.

He kept on looking at the patient to check his condition and make sure he hadn't come round fully. It was then he made a decision to replace the file in the briefcase, which he slotted beneath the stretcher, intending to leave it there, inadvertently of course, until after they'd admitted the patient. Once he had the opportunity to slip the case notes out and into his car he'd returned the briefcase to Casualty. They were so busy that his little plan worked.

Now that he'd got his hands on the notes, more particularly the valuable statements, how about if he put the skids under Ritchie? The witness statements could remain as they were for a price, and he'd see to it that the file was returned to the solicitor. No-one would be any the wiser. Failing Ritchie's co-operation he could threaten to drop him in it.

But his plan hadn't worked out the way he had hoped. He'd approached

Ritchie and promised to keep the matter of the witnesses to himself provided Ritchie cut him in on some of the winnings. But Ritchie had called his bluff. He hadn't believed O'Brien would do such a thing. He certainly hadn't accounted for his contacting Bickerdyke & Wagstaff.

And now what use was the file? As far as O'Brien was concerned the statements would be invalid once it was established they had been forged. Did he dispose of the file containing the testimonies by placing it in a litter bin, or did he return it to the solicitors? After the anonymous phone call letting the firm of solicitors know the truth about the statements, he would follow it up by sending the file to them in the post. They could check out the couple and prove that Ritchie had been lying. That would put Ritchie in an invidious position. Who would want to represent him then?

That was a couple of weeks ago and he still had the folder.

Kevin returned from the station. He was tired. It had been a hard day but he must go out once more. The guy from the solicitors had been sniffing around at the ambulance station and it seemed they were getting closer to discovering the whereabouts of the missing file.

He switched on his laptop, copied the name of the solicitors on to a label, stuck it on to a large envelope and slipped the file inside. He took his leather jacket from behind the door and put it on, leaving the house and making for the post office in the city centre.

After paying the postage, the clerk slipped the envelope into a large postal sack. That way they'd not be able to check on its source. And he needn't worry about fingerprints. He'd been careful when handling the documents not to touch them without wearing hospital issue latex gloves, firstly in the ambulance and afterwards at home. If Ritchie didn't want to play ball then he would suffer the consequences.

Brian Ritchie was livid. His plan had

been thwarted — and by his so-called friend, Kevin O'Brien. There was no doubt about it. Kev had changed since his wife had left him. But he didn't blame her for leaving. O'Brien didn't know he was on to a good thing with Karen. She was a lovely girl, so attractive and caring. But Kevin had to play around.

Ritchie couldn't understand it. They'd been so devoted at first. And in these days Kev had been the life and soul of the party. But no more.

After Karen left him he became bitter. He was jealous, especially when he heard about the lottery win. If O'Brien thought he could get away with shopping him to the solicitors he could think again.

Ritchie decided to lie in wait until O'Brien returned for the night and settle the dispute once and for all. He knew O'Brien was on the middle shift and would be home around eight o'clock by which time it was getting dark.

He spotted the green Jaguar turning the corner into the road and coming to a standstill outside O'Brien's house. Now was his chance. O'Brien stepped out of his car, locked it and walked down the drive towards the front door. As he placed the key in the lock, Ritchie came up behind him and hit him on the head with a heavy stick. O'Brien fell to the ground, clutching his head and groaning.

Ritchie didn't want to cause any serious damage, and he saw that O'Brien was still conscious. He didn't wait around to see what happened after that. He managed to slip away unnoticed. An eye for an eye — that was Ritchie's policy.

Rosie was on duty when they brought O'Brien into Casualty. He had a deep laceration to the side of the head and he seemed to be delirious. His partner, Alan, had found him. O'Brien had left his mobile phone in the ambulance and Alan had dashed across to return it.

It was lucky for O'Brien. The gash

was bleeding and he needed stitches in the wound. Between them Dr Holgate and Rosie managed to stem the bleeding. They stitched the gash and sent O'Brien to one of the wards pending further investigations.

It was when Rosie came on duty the following day that she was called into the office by Sister Wilson. 'I've had a strange request, Rosie. Kevin O'Brien, the ambulance attendant has asked to see you. He's on ward five.'

'Yes, I knew he was there. We admitted him yesterday with a very bad gash on his head. We had to keep him in to give him a thorough check up. But why does he want a word with me?'

'I've no idea but we're quiet just now. Pop along and see him, but don't be long.'

Rosie couldn't imagine why Kevin should wish to speak with her. But she was determined to be strong and not to let anything get to her.

He was sitting up in bed when she entered the ward. His head was

159

bandaged and she thought he was looking rather serious and thoroughly dejected. 'Please sit down, Rosie,' he said. 'There's something I want to say to you.'

Rosie took a seat beside the bed and replied, 'I hope you're feeling better Kevin. What on earth happened?'

'A friend of mine, well I used to call him a friend, attacked me.'

'But why should a friend attack you?'

'It's a long story. But that's not why I asked to talk to you.' He took a deep breath. 'First of all thanks for what you and the doc did for me yesterday. I have my mate, Alan, to thank too.'

He hesitated before he continued. 'Most of all I want to apologise. I've been a stupid idiot. I confess I did fancy you,' he smiled, 'I still do, but I shouldn't have gone to the lengths I did to spite you, just because you refused my advances. I only did it in fun to start with, anyway. But I suppose you deflated me, just when I needed a bit of a boost. Sorry if I frightened you on the reservoir path.'

'So it was you, Kevin. I thought as much when I saw you with your car in the lay-by. It was your car in the reservoir car park that morning, wasn't it?'

'It was. But I hadn't gone there to frighten you again. I'd gone to explain to you how sorry I was. When you turned up with another three people I left.'

'That's my normal routine to walk with my friends. The day I walked alone was a one-off.' Rosie shook her head. 'I just don't understand what got into you to do such a thing.' She paused. 'I don't suppose you had anything to do with the knock on my door or the note on my car.'

'Guilty again, Rosie. I don't know what got into me either. But it won't happen again, I promise you.'

'The warden persuaded me to report the stalking. You realise the police know.'

'I had no idea it had been reported.'

He closed his eyes momentarily. 'But no harm came to you, so surely they will drop any charges. I can't afford to be accused of that sort of thing. I could lose my job.'

'If you promise me nothing like this will ever happen again, I'll drop the complaint. But I can't promise the police won't drop their investigations. The warden was concerned for the safety of other people, especially children.'

'I would never harm anyone. And you have my word, Rosie. It will never happen again. I'm so sorry.' Embarrassed, he turned his head away.

'I understand, Kevin. But you must realise it's no longer in my hands. You'll just have to hope the police drop it.' There was no harm in making him sweat. It was wrong of him to frighten her so, and on so many different occasions. But she certainly wouldn't pursue things with the police now that Kevin had confessed.

Kevin took a deep breath and turned

to face her again. 'By the way, I'd like a word with that boyfriend of yours. I've something else to confess. I may as well get it all off my chest.'

'Boyfriend? I suppose you mean Sam. He's not my boyfriend, he's just a friend. But I'll get a message to him. He'll no doubt come along here and have a word with you.'

Rosie decided not to mention anything to the others about O'Brien's confession. She firmly believed he would stick to his promise. Perhaps the assault by his so-called friend had been his comeuppance, his punishment.

It was going to be tricky contacting Sam and asking him to visit Kevin O'Brien in hospital. And what on earth he wanted to see Sam about she'd no idea. But it was not her business any longer. Perhaps if she telephoned the company and had a word with his secretary she could pass the message on to Sam.

The others were waiting when Rosie drew up in the car park for the walk.

They were all smiling as she stepped out from her car.

'I must say, you're looking rather smug,' she observed. 'Is there something I should know?' she added.

Emma held out her hand and flashed a lovely diamond solitaire before turning around and looking up at Rick.

'Does this mean what I think it means?' Rosie asked.

'Emma and I are engaged to be married,' Rick told her, slipping his arm around Emma's waist. 'We haven't told anyone until now but we've been going out for months.'

'Months? How come I didn't know before?'

'We wanted to keep it a secret until Rick was promoted. He was expecting it, but not so early,' Emma explained.

'Then congratulations,' Rosie replied, pulling the two of them close and giving them both a peck on the cheek. 'I'm sure you'll be very happy together,' she continued, again feeling guilty that she had ever thought Rick could have been the stalker, when all the time he was set on nothing more than protecting her.

Rick and Emma set out in front of them. Abby and Rosie fell behind.

'Now we know why they've arrived together each morning,' Abby whispered. 'Hey, you two, when are you getting married?' she called out.

Emma turned to them. 'Don't worry we'll let you know, all in good time.'

Rosie began to think about her own situation. Another two weeks and she would be forced to meet up with Imran. She hoped he would understand. She couldn't explain anything to him. Not that there was anything to explain now that she'd broken off her flimsy relationship with Sam. But it didn't change her feelings about him.

She'd missed him since they parted, but she was too proud to go back on her word. That would have been her only solution. And she concluded that she couldn't possibly switch her feelings to some other man.

9

It was the day after Rosie had passed on the message from O'Brien to Sam's secretary. The phone rang. It was Sam.

'Hello, Rosie. I've missed you — you know that, don't you?'

'Not really, Sam. Not when you suspected me of stealing a folder from your brief case.'

'What on earth are you talking about, Rosie? I never said anything of the sort.'

'I know you didn't, but that was the inference.'

'Please see me, Rosie. There's so much we have to talk about.'

'I don't think that would be wise.'

'And why not?'

'It's time, Sam. It's next week when I meet Imran. What am I going to do?'

'Imran? You mean the 'intended'?'

Rosie shook her head. The name floating around in her mind was not

Imran but 'Egghead', but she was being unkind again, especially since she'd never even met the guy. 'That's right. And you know my feelings about meeting up with him,' she replied.

Sam seemed to hesitate. 'But you've no alternative, Rosie. You must go through with it, if only for your parents' sake. You said they've agreed to give you time to become fully acquainted with each other. And to be fair, failing any spark between you, they have inserted a let-out clause,' he added, using his legal jargon to convince her it was the right thing to do. 'The agreement can be broken on either side. He may be feeling the same — for all you know.'

'It's not as easy as that. It's so embarrassing having to go through the motions of introductions and then getting to know someone when I'm not ready for this. I'm not ready for marriage, certainly not with Imran.'

'I see. You are ready for marriage then, but to someone else,' he suggested, and Rosie detected a kind of gleeful enthusiasm in his voice.

'That's not what I said, Sam,' she snapped.

'OK. Say no more, Rosie. We could go on all day. And you're only becoming more and more stressed by dwelling on it. The subject's closed. How about if you come over here and we have a take-away at my place?'

'You mean the Last Supper,' Rosie replied, a sorrowful edge to her voice. 'I don't think so. We'd only be going over the same things again and again.'

'Not necessarily. And you could listen to me. I've so much I want to tell you.'

'Sorry. I've made up my mind. Thanks but, no thanks.'

'But you will keep in touch, won't you, Rosie?' he begged.

'I'll try. I must go now, Sam. Goodbye,' she concluded, finding the strength to replace the receiver.

But that wasn't the end of it. He called her again the following day, and the day after that, and it was obvious that if she wasn't prepared to keep in touch, he was.

'How are you feeling today, Rosie?' he asked her.

'Just the same,' she told him, her voice a monotone.

'You should hear yourself,' Sam said, laughing. 'You sound like a puppy dog who's had her biscuit taken away. Snap out of it, love.'

It was fine Sam telling her to snap out of it. He wasn't the one going through this charade. But what would she gain by being miserable? It was the last time she'd speak to Sam before she met up with Imran the following day.

She lightened up and when it was time for him to ring off, she gave him one last chance to tell her how he felt about her. Goodness knows she knew beneath all the bravado how she felt about him, but she wasn't about to tell him that.

'Oh, Sam,' she whispered. 'I don't know if I can go through with this.'

'You must, Rosie. Give it a chance.

Who knows, you two might get on like a house on fire.'

'No, we won't,' she stressed, bitterly disappointed that Sam could think such a thing.

'Then maybe I know why,' Sam replied.

Rosie was silent for a moment. But still Sam didn't tell her how he felt. It was as though he was backing off. 'But let's not get into anything complicated,' he begged. 'See how it goes. But don't forget me, Rosie, whatever the outcome.'

Rosie was puzzled that Sam hadn't made more effort. Perhaps he didn't feel the pull between them as she did. Alternatively he could be feeling quietly confident that she would reject Imran — in his favour. That was conceited of him. But there was no way she would rush back to Sam when it didn't work out with Imran.

Whatever Sam's feelings, he hadn't tried to keep their relationship going the way she would have done had the reverse happened. But maybe he was doing it this way to protect her from any more disappointment and stress. Maybe he was doing it out of kindness.

She was feeling more depressed than ever now. Why hadn't he made a fuss? Was this really the end with Sam?

Rosie set off directly from the hospital on Friday evening after her shift which finished at six. She'd packed her weekend case and taken it with her that morning. It was always a nightmare travelling back to Birmingham on Fridays whatever the time of day. If she had a decent start, she should make it in a couple of hours.

So much for Sam seeing her off! He was walking without the sticks now and it would have been no hardship for him to pop down to Casualty at five-thirty after he finished work. But he obviously didn't want to become involved or feel he was in the way.

He knew what arranged marriages meant to parents of the older genera-tion, even though so many of today's younger generation were given choices. If there was someone else who was acceptable to the parents and of the same faith they would often negotiate. But Sam hadn't given her that opportunity. He'd made no effort to tell her how he felt.

Her parents were excited when she arrived at the house.

'We have everything ready, Rosie. Imran is coming tomorrow at eleven. Your father and I would like the two of you to talk things through. We'll leave you together in the lounge.'

'That's fine, Mum,' Rosie replied, a complete lack of enthusiasm in her voice. 'But you can't expect me to make a decision after one solitary meeting. I'll need to get to know Imran a little more before I can tell you how I feel.'

'We appreciate that, darling,' Asad Khan told his daughter, 'and we've arranged for Imran to stay with your Uncle Khalid for the weekend. That way you'll have plenty of time to spend together. And you will give it a fair chance, won't you? I'm sure you two will get on. Imran's parents were always our best friends, when we were much younger, of course, and there's no reason why he won't be every bit as kind and caring as they were.'

'Point taken, Dad. But being kind and caring isn't everything, is it? Not when it's someone you'll be spending the rest of your life with.'

'But it's a start. That's the way it was with your mother and I. Granted, we had known each other since we were children, having been brought up in the same village.'

'Exactly, Dad,' she replied.

The time dragged. Rosie's father went round to Uncle Khalid's place and brought him back for dinner.

'We're immensely proud of you, Rosina,' Uncle Khalid told her. 'This match between you and Imran is what we've waited for since you were a child. You're not like some of the modern daughters who rebel. You are a credit to our family and our culture.'

Rosie felt she was being drawn deeper and deeper into this argument. But what could she do?

'You see, Rosina, it is usual for parents to choose a partner from within the family, but your father and I, as children, were the only family survivors after the earthquake. Practically the whole village was lost. But your mother survived and our good friend, Imran — Senior of course — and Shazia. And that's when it all started. We were survivors, and we felt we belonged to each other. We were a family.'

Rosie looked at her parents and she saw the tears in their eyes.

'I remember father telling me about the earthquake when I was a little girl, but I didn't realise there were so few survivors,' Rosie admitted.

'Even as children your mother and father, and Imran and Shazia, vowed that when they married their children would be betrothed. They were so close, they wanted this 'family' tie to continue.'

Rosie swallowed hard. How could she deny them their dreams? As children, they'd each of them struggled for survival. How could she be so selfish? If she married Imran it would make their dreams come true.

'I understand, Uncle Khalid. I won't let you down,' she promised, now more than ever determined to make it work.

When Rosie stepped out of bed the following morning her nerves began to get the better of her. She dreaded the appearance of this Imran person, whoever he was. But maybe he was a bag of nerves too.

Ten minutes to eleven and the door bell sounded. Rosie couldn't bear to look out of the window, but the flash of a car caught her eye and she turned slightly, noticing a taxi speeding away.

'Come in, Shazia,' she heard her mother cry. 'It's lovely to see you again after all this time. And we've waited so long to meet Imran.'

'It's so wonderful to see you too. This is my son, Imran. He was only three years old the last time you met him.' The comment was followed by suppressed laughter.

'Do come in, Imran,' Rosie heard her mother cry. 'You're the image of your father.' There was a clapping of hands. 'Shazia, what a handsome son you have.'

When she heard footsteps in the hall, Rosie moved to the edge of the sofa. And when she looked up she saw the door handle turning. This was it. Her stomach started to somersault.

The door opened and her father entered the room.

'They're here at last, Rosina.' He turned and took the hand of a very attractive woman who stepped into the room. 'Shazia, this is our daughter, Rosina,' he added and the woman offered her hand. 'Rosina meet Imran's mother,' he concluded.

'I've waited so long to meet you, too. I've never seen you of course, but I have seen photographs.' She smiled and turned to Asad and Serina. 'You have a beautiful daughter.'

Rosie heard her mother's tiny laugh of appreciation as she popped her head around the door. 'A cup of tea, Shazia,' she said as she hovered in the doorway.

'That would be lovely, Serina,' Shazia replied. 'We'll leave the young ones to get to know each other.' She turned and left the room.

Rosie's father stepped into the room. 'Rosina, darling, I'd like you to meet Imran.'

Rosie couldn't believe her eyes. She closed them momentarily and opened them again. Her parents left the room.

'But, Sam, it's you,' she cried. 'I don't understand.'

'Nor did I until a few days ago,' Sam declared, opening his arms and pulling her close. He kissed her gently and added, 'Sit down and I'll explain. And perhaps we'd better behave until things are finalised.' He laughed and Rosie shook her head in sheer disbelief.

Sam released her and continued. 'It was when you were going on about the liaison the following week that you dropped the name Imran. That's my middle name and the one used by my parents since I was a child. You see it was my father's name too. And of course, all their friends and family have used that name since.'

'But why have you never told me that name?'

'When I started at university everyone called me by the name that comes first on my birth certificate and my passport, Samir. I became used to it, and my friends started to call me Sam. I rather liked that. By then I didn't see any reason to change back to Imran. My full name is Samir Imran Azam. Of course when I was a boy I was Imran junior and my father was Imran senior.'

'But didn't they ever call you Samir, or Sam even — for short?'

'No. I was always Imran. And Sam would have been too European for them. They wanted me to keep my roots.'

'But you didn't tell me that things

were arranged for you, Sam.' Rosie was hurt that he hadn't confided in her.

'I thought we had enough pressures without me telling you of my circumstances as well. And to be honest I've tried to duck out of my responsibilities since I came to England. I had the same feelings as you. I didn't want an arranged marriage. But my father made me promise before he died that I would carry out his wishes. It was very difficult for me to deny them.'

'I know what you mean, Sam. It's that feeling of disloyalty if you go against their wishes. But once you knew it was me, why didn't you tell me?' Rosie was wide-eyed with curiosity.

'I had literally five days' notice from my mother that I was to meet you. When she told me your full name, I just couldn't believe it. She had mentioned your name in the past but it had never sunk in, simply because I didn't want to know.'

'It's all falling into place now,' Rosie told him as he pulled her close.

'I was elated when I realised it was you. I did invite you over. I told you I had things to discuss with you, but you turned me down. I didn't want to tell you over the phone because you'd gone off me. I needed to see you face to face.'

His brow creased into a frown. 'And especially after the few weeks we've had with you accusing me of accusing you, so to speak!' He shook his head. 'Why did you carry it on, Rosie? You knew it wasn't true.'

'I didn't realise it at the time but I think it must have been psychological. I had to have an excuse to stop seeing you. That, I suppose, was it.'

'I see now that you've explained. And by the way, the guy I went to see, Kevin O'Brien has confessed he took the folder. But he did us a favour in the end. He's convinced us Ritchie's two witness statements were forged.'

'That must have been what happened. The other guy must have found out and attacked him,' Rosie replied, and Sam's reference to Kevin O'Brien triggered off thoughts of the stalking. But there was no point in telling Sam about that now. He might retaliate. He might contact O'Brien again. And she didn't want that. It was too late — it was sorted.

'Yes, that's right, Rosie.' Sam took her hand in his. 'But to get back to us — you and me. At the time I was devastated you'd taken things the wrong way.'

'I'm sorry, Sam. It was just that I felt so hurt. And then one thing led to another. But I must admit I thought you were letting me go without a fight when you didn't come to see me before I left.'

'I had to do that. Things happened so quickly, what with Mother contacting me and telling me she was on her way over. And I wasn't absolutely sure it was you until I phoned your parents again on Thursday evening.'

'So they knew too. Why has everyone been so secretive?' she asked, her face now wearing a sulky look.

'Come off it, Rosie. It's only been a matter of days.'

'And how much did you know about your own arrangements?'

'Very little actually. I've been burying my head in the sand ever since I started at university. But I knew that one day I'd have to succumb.'

'Didn't your parents give you a choice?' Rosie asked him.

'I'm afraid not. Having promised my father when he was on his death bed that I'd follow it through, I had no alternative although, to be fair, Mother did say the final decision was mine. But like you, inside I just couldn't accept it. And that's why I didn't take in your name, except that I was told your parents were called Khan. But since it's not exactly rare to be called Khan, I never made the link.'

'I can't believe it, Sam. After all this time, dreading meeting the highly-intelligent, over-qualified, wonderful Imran — I'm quoting my parents of course — I've finally met you. You've no idea the image I had in my mind of this 'mummy's boy'. My secret name for him was Egghead.'

Sam started to laugh. He took her hands once more and drew her towards him. 'Egghead? And what do you think now? Do you still regard me as a brainbox?'

'Of course I do, but not in the way I first thought.'

'And talking of mummy's boy, we need to let her know everything has worked out for the best. She'll need to vet my bride-to-be.'

'Hang on a minute. You haven't proposed yet.'

Sam slid off the sofa, and knelt before her.

'My darling Rosie. I love you with all my heart. Will you marry me?' He took hold of her hands and squeezed them.

Rosie took a deep breath and stared into his eyes. She knew for certain she was somehow inextricably drawn to him. There was something about him that delighted her immensely. She had always enjoyed being in his company and now she knew the feeling was mutual.

She drew him to his feet, pulled him towards her and kissed him gently on the lips.

'I love you too, Sam. And my answer is yes.'

THE END

We do hope that you have enjoyed reading this large print book.

Did you know that all of our titles are available for purchase?

We publish a wide range of high quality large print books including:
Romances, Mysteries, Classics
General Fiction
Non Fiction and Westerns

Special interest titles available in large print are:
The Little Oxford Dictionary
Music Book, Song Book
Hymn Book, Service Book

Also available from us courtesy of Oxford University Press:
Young Readers' Dictionary
(large print edition)
Young Readers' Thesaurus
(large print edition)

For further information or a free brochure, please contact us at:
Ulverscroft Large Print Books Ltd.,
The Green, Bradgate Road, Anstey,
Leicester, LE7 7FU, England.
Tel: (00 44) **0116 236 4325**
Fax: (00 44) **0116 234 0205**

FELICITY MOON

Valerie Holmes

When, in self defence, Felicity Moon strikes her employer Julian Cannon, she is forced to leave the place where her father had sent her for her own safety. Accused and jailed for bank-rolling smugglers, Squire Moon is unaware of the dangers Felicity is facing. She is given one last chance by Cannon's housekeeper in the form of a reference to Mr Lucas Packman, a man her father distrusts. Felicity faces a stark choice: trust Packman or her father.